An Assassin's Quest

Book 2

The fall and Rise of Merr StahlRhune

Author

By Lez Lewis

Lez Lewis

Published by

ARTEAZE Inc.

Cover and Art by

Kindred Muse

Edited by

Tunapeppers

July 2011

ISBN

978-0-9866345-5-0

Something of whom and what has gone before

Merr StahlRhune awoke knowing only her name and age, but soon found herself enslaved in the household of Mistress Copper. Events proceeded through ritualized sessions and instructions, taking her name from her and replacing it with Copper's Doll, as well as indoctrinating her into a culture of sex magic and utter submission.

All but Mistress Copper are slaves and all are happy with their position. These include Toy, Crap, Hex, Pepper, Sugar and Cum all ruled by Mistress Copper. Soon another, Taken, joined the house. After a dangerous evening in the local watering hole, the HFC or Hell Fire Club, assisted by a strong mercenary, Slice, who later became attached to the household as a hire sword and able lover, we meet Mistress Copper's demonic 'First Girl', Spite who successfully drags a captured assailant back to hell to be her slave.

Lez Lewis

Authors Signing Page

Chapter One

Macey stands there wrapped in shadows watching and waiting, patiently waiting for the one she has been summoned to deal with. She is barely visible in the half light and at least partly concealed by both a spell and a magical cloak. Taller than most humans she is enshrouded in the creeping dimness of the encroaching night, standing stock still, alone her sky blue skin is barely visible on her face and hands. Where seen her skin is in striking contrast to the wisps of her red hair, black talons, eyes and hooves. The armor she wears came straight from hell, a combination of ceramic, bone and horn; it is lighter, harder and quieter than any mortal armor ever made. But this armor is mostly covered by her cloak, a cloak that is not only stylish but also covers her in a suitably modest and decent fashion. This magical weave conjured in hell seems to bend the light around itself making the wearer appear to fold and blend into any background she finds herself in front of.

Her mortal brother Malthus has summoned her from her home on the plane of hell of Niffelem. Not that the two of them have ever been particularly close or even very trusting of each other but she needs him to cast the spell of summoning to bring her up to London, just as he needs her strength and the magic she brings up from hell. This time though is different, special for her, she is not just bringing magical items or the ether

1

from the fields of hell but she has been summoned specifically to rip the soul from an offensive little whore.

For him, she shrugs it is probably just politics or perhaps revenge. For her, there is a soul to steal, a soul to savor, just as a human would lust after the finest feast in London so she lusts after the delight of tearing a soul from the body of a depraved human. Her brother would not use hookers even if he could. No the girl must have found some other way to run afoul of her brother or perhaps she is loved by one of his enemies. But that simply does not matter, to feast on a soul now that is the only thing that really matters! Savoring that final pleasant thought her good humor drops away as she recognizes her prey. There are five mortals in all, two men one strong and well-armed but a collared slave none the less, and the other appears to be a free warrior. The warrior saunters at the side of her brother's sworn enemy, the tall red haired whore called Mistress Copper. Two other slaves follow, one garbed in long robes walking with the distinctive grace and style of a high level spell caster, that slave appears to barely touch the ground somehow seeming to glide rather than lowering herself to take a step, but the one who is in the middle, she is the prey. She appears to be a very young busty blond, quite well outfitted and strutting proudly in the armor only a true Succubus whore would don. This girl is wearing a collar with chains linked to her nipples and below, a collar that reads Copper's Doll. Macey inhales deeply and marks the girl's face, form and position for now she has seen her prearranged target. Allowing a low frustrated growl from deep in her throat seep past her lips, Macey also knows that this will not be as easy as expected. Had the copper haired whore left her target behind in the house well then perhaps she might be a bit more vulnerable, traps and surprises in the house notwithstanding. But now with all five at full guard the task is nearly impossible.

Waiting while they pass and then waiting still longer, she sees another slink from the same door. A short platinum blonde wearing a similar sort of light cloak as Macey wears. This one slips and flicks through the shadows like a hand in a glove, this slave walks as only a thief would, she is barely visible as she moves to follow the rest. Pleased that she has found the rear guard, Macey silently slips in behind this last hidden impediment. Her tall blue form moves like a shadow through the evening, horns held high and tail coiled out of the way smiling just enough for her black fangs to peek between her lips. The blue demon slides along the shadowed walls almost unseen by all.

But not quite all failed to mark her passage for after the demon has moved, two more figures emerge from the same door as the preceding six. Two figures each are carrying a black bladed sword that sucks even the failing light of the sun into its self. These two have their own prey; they are intent on the elimination of the demonic presence that stalks those they love. The collars they wear identify them as slaves of Mistress Copper, Copper's Taken and Copper's Pepper. They had not really been prepared for this as the white flour still on Pepper's hands and clothing attests. Neither of these two moves with the stealth or the grace of the others but with determination written across their faces that is as firm as their grips on the black swords they hold. Moving quickly to overtake the blue demoness their lack of stealth is soon noticed.

Macey upon hearing the threat behind her quickly moves. Her tall blue body slips around a corner only to be met by a sword stabbing towards her belly. Twisting herself aside at the last instant, she avoids the worst of the thrust but gasps in pain as the unexpected black sword bites hard into her side, barely missing her belly. She hisses in pain and indignation as the sword thrust from Copper's Sugar opens a gash along her side. The black metal edge of the sword does not just cut, the enchanted metal wrenches at her very life force dragging it bit by bit through the gash.

Her attacker has crowded too close to allow her to use her trident but undeterred her demonic claws flash out, black talons gripping and piercing deep into Sugar's throat. Dragging the thief's face close to her own, looking into the small thief's eyes, she smiles as the red blood gushes between her fingers. Snarling and barring her fangs while staring directly into the eyes of the strangling girl, her tail tears the hated black demon blade from the thief's hand. Laughing with demonic glee, Macey's talons tear and pierce deeply into Sugar's throat as the blood of the human mixes with her own smoking black demonic blood on the cobblestone roadway.

The piercing ripping pain returns with a vengeance as another black blade stabs deeply into her back. Throwing the white haired slave into the wall Macey spins to find herself faced by the slaves, Pepper and Taken. Jumping back and steeling herself to the pain of the wound, she pulls her trident from a loop. Ignoring the magical threat of the black blade, she lunges into a slashing attack from Pepper. With practiced skill, the tall blue demoness allows the black blade to slash between the tines of her trident; this allows her to end this threat by twisting and flipping her trident, ripping the black magical blade from the slave's hand. But she has only been partly successful for Taken's black blade slashes into her already bleeding, unguarded side. Weakened, bleeding badly from the two sword wounds in her side and a deep wound to her back, Macey swings wildly with her trident, allowing Pepper to dive below it grasping at her sword. In this instant of respite between attacks Macey staggers back, stealing the moment from her attackers. The demoness motions and utters a word of power that heals her ragged wounds. But at this same dreadful instant she also sees and hears Taken speak an erotic word and make an obscene gesture. As her wounds heal, she also feels the disgusting 'Spell of Seduction' settle over her encompassing her thoughts like a blanket. Yoked irrevocably to Taken that whorish mortal, Macey reels out of control. She is overcome by a wanton need for the mortal. The unholy perversion she feels for the slave

4

overwhelms all her mind and body, she must give herself to this slave. Unbelievably she wants to kneel in supplication before the wretch. Unable to prevent it, she feels the mortal grab her and brutally force her to her knees.

This, the most hateful spell of all has trapped her. In a lifetime of good, highly moralistic activities plus many more mortal lifetimes as a demoness, she never strayed from the path of purity. Her love and her life dedicated to sexual exclusivity! Just her and only one other or at least until in a long forgotten random battle she rode the highway to hell but this spell, the 'Spell of Seduction' steals all that away. Macey, the Inquisitor demoness finds herself placed in a magically induced state that makes her need for the spell caster's passions paramount even though it falls to the most sickening and repugnant of outcomes. The disgust she feels for this filthy lewdness cannot overcome the magic that fills her mind, warping her very reason for being. As the spell wraps its twisted morality into her mind she feels the overpowering lust for this foul enchantress. This is against all she knows of being right and good. This obscenely overwhelming desire to be held, be used, abused and degraded by Taken overshadows all of her moral codes. This can only be denigration incarnate. Even the knowledge that the desires running through her now are the result of a 'Seduction Spell', even knowing that she is about to be attacked, she drops her cloak peeling off her armor as she pleads indecently to the spell caster, not for mercy but to be used like a cheap whore. Yet from somewhere deep inside a demonic rage grows, a rage focused into hatred of the one who has so enthralled her.

Pleading to be used, she sees both of her attackers step forward holding their swords ready to rend her but rather than the black blades stabbing she hears the spell binder command her to answer.

Taken secure in the knowledge that the kneeling demoness is of no immediate threat, places the tip of her black bladed sword on the exposed blue throat. With casual intensity she asks, "Why do you hunt those of Mistress Copper's house?"

As she looks up at the one she has been seduced by she involuntarily runs her talons up and down between the blue black lips of the furrow between her thighs; Macey tries to evade the question by plunging her talon tipped finger deep inside herself. Still she has no choice, she must answer honestly, "My brother Malthus summoned me to cut the heart and soul out of the one called 'Copper's Doll'. The rest of you do not matter to him but it is my nature to hunt the souls of the fallen mortals." Feeling her basic essence losing the war with her desperation to be used, she begs again groveling before the mortal. "Please use me as you will! I can't help myself! Please!"

More out of pity than from anger Taken inhales deeply before transferring her weight to the sword which slides effortlessly into that demonic throat and down into the chest of the demoness. On her knees Macey has no defense, but as her black blood and the coppery taste of death rush into her mouth she just has the time for one last thought, "I came for one! But I shall return for you!"

The demoness's steamy black blood pools under her fallen body, the two panting slaves stand over it seeing her blue skin turn an even darker bluer in death. They know that this body is dead but they also know full well that the demoness that had inhabited it has been returned to hell. If only for a day London is safe from her again.

Hearing a barely audible gasp both of the slaves turn to see the horror of the attack their sister endured. Pepper cradles Sugar's shoulders holding her sister tightly; she uses a silk scarf as a bandage pressing it into place over the torn throat. Taken turns and dashes in a full out run to find her Mistress. But for Sugar lying in the arms of her sister, the pain fades as

6

all turns into blackness. Pepper holding her sister tightly, croons softly, her tears falling to land and mix with the immortal demonic blood and the blood of her now dying sister.

In a different part of London, Malthus standing over a newly capture beastling whore, suddenly looks up with the realization that his sister has been returned to hell. Knowing that this must mean her defeat at the hands of the copper haired whore, his lips peel back exposing his teeth in a grim parody of a smile. Snarling at the beastling and with far more passion than is required, he drives his ritual knife into the whore's body, carving through her ribs and finally cutting the heart free from her chest. Reveling in the power he has gained but still not pleased as his plans for the day have gone horribly wrong.

Two sets of hidden eyes also witnessed the fight, eyes that have watched all. One set of eyes sees differently than the other. Through the gleaming red eyes of the nightingale everything is sharp and clear but totally without color. For the other set, frozen in stillness, peaking from between narrow alley walls the sight is less clear. Cyril hiding concealed in a tight alley which most Londoners could not squeeze into, finds that his vision is constricted and limited not only by the walls but also by the cowled hem of his concealment cloak. But what he does see puzzles and troubles him greatly.

The assassin-thief Sugar has fallen in battle. Why she attacked is not really clear but shows her great loyalty to her Mistress. Possibly it was not the smartest thing to do but any human that attacks any demon alone, has to be feared. This is a troubling thing, for this is the same girl that has been asking after him. Several people have told him that he is the one she has been seeking.

But the 'Why' is the puzzlement? He has never stolen from any of the House of Copper, nor is he so vain as to believe that a simple thief like himself could be found desirable by this awesome white haired assassin. She is nearly a legend in her own right, he is a simple pickpocket whose greatest valor is to occasionally pop a lock or steal a kiss along with a pouch of coins. This bit of reality combined with seeing one of London's most feared assassin-thieves being ripped apart by a demoness is not only puzzling but really scary. No! Right now! Right here! And as of this moment, Cyril decides he really, really wants nothing to do with this mess, with Sugar or her family. Fingering his own throat he winces and returns to rigid stillness as he hears others returning.

Mistress Copper hearing the sounds of fighting behind her rushes back to the confrontation. She arrives first meeting Taken who has been running to find her then seeing a dead Inquisitress demoness beside a kneeling Pepper. But held in Pepper's arms is her darling Sugar bleeding freely from deep punctures on her throat. Both are surrounded by a widening pool of blood. Mistress Copper and Hex as one, cast their greatest spells of healing while rushing to the fallen thief.

Slice, Cum and I form a defensive wall around the Mistress and Sugar. Mistress Copper takes Sugar in her arms and cries out in rage at seeing the scaring of five punctures wounds. Pepper, Hex and Taken join us in standing guard over the healer and the fallen. Sugar, blood drenched, with the new scars on her throat groans as her eyes open. But somehow even the groan sounds wrong. The pitch of the groan comes out very high. When she tries to speak, trying to reassure Mistress and the others, the true extend of the demonic damage is revealed. For where there was once a rich sweet voice, the words she now speaks come as almost a squeak. Sugar's face drops and her eyes and mouth open wide in shock, disbelief and panic. Her pain, her horror, her damaged voice, all these pile onto her until in surrender she slumps fainting into her Mistress's lap.

Lifting Sugar into her arms with a grim face and carrying her slave Mistress Copper walks stiffly back toward her home. She strokes and soothes her wounded slave murmuring and reassuring the unconscious girl as she hugs her tightly. She wastes not a glance away from Sugar trusting completely to her family for total protection. She focuses on Sugar alone. The rest of us follow at full alert all now so angry that any attackers would be welcomed with fire, steel, spells and no quarter given or asked. Slice seeing how desperate the situation is and how much haste is needed looks at Taken saying, "Don't forget your trophies girl, I'll help you carry the armor". He then proceeds to toss the demonic armor onto the fallen cloak, wrapping and carrying it as Taken grabs the trident.

Leading off in front, Slice, Hex and Taken prowl for any hint of an enemy, Cum and I behind, walking backwards ready to repel any attack. I have never felt so alive, every nerve, every fiber of my being enraged and at full alert. The bond of the brand burning into me brings me to total awareness of Mistress and her desire to heal Sugar. The deep rage Mistress feels towards whoever is responsible for this is a pure white hot fire. Mistress wants blood, barrels of it on the streets and she wants the skull of one called Malthus mounted as a door knocker. I could also sense Mistress's suspicions that we have been betrayed and will momentarily be attacked by an overwhelming force. All this I know because of the link from my brand.

This awareness of Mistress's need spurs my senses to search again. I find myself looking out with my mind as I would normally look out with my eyes. Searching by feelings alone, I try to identify and find all friends or foes around me. I partly see, partly feel a malevolent presence. Without a second thought, in a perfectly practiced motion, I place one foot slightly behind the other, pivot on that heel, raising my wand. I don't even have to aim I know exactly where the spy is and let fly a blast from my wand. A hit! Solid and hard!

One watcher has died, one set of eyes will never see again, for there is a short squawk followed by the crackle of burning feathers as a nightingale falls from a window ledge. That watcher is now nothing but a charred lump on the cobblestones. Hex glancing over, first at the mess then back to me, nods in appreciation; she casts and I feel the rush of power that signals the magical enhancement creating strengths where weakness had been. I am on fire now every pore is alive, aware and searching for another kill. Hex glides to the smoking carcass and reaches down, picking up something small and gold, snarling, "Not all spies walk, some like that one fly from parts unknown."

I feel the surging of energies coursing through me; I feel stronger, smarter and faster than before. Before I had been angry wishing for a foe, now I will embrace a fight with the glee of a berserker in full rage. I search from right to left, from road to sky, continually scanning for the tiniest of movements that would signal an attack. I stand alone still searching but as the rest of the guards have entered Cum drags me back through the door.

Cyril slowly lets out the air from his lungs, the breath he had forgotten he was holding. The deadly display of the blond with the wand scares him enough to cause sweat to run down between his shoulder blades. Her reaction was incredible to have seen. Pure poetry of motion and total economy of action has resulted in a totally unexpected execution. He had not seen the other watcher; moreover, in the dim light he really doubted that the girl had either. He was not sure how she had made the shot even though he had seen it with his own eyes. He was certain there was just as good a chance that he could have been identified as a watcher as well. Waiting until the door has slammed behind the blond, he follows his first instinct and slides from the alley running in the opposite direction.

Hearing a door open he looks behind him and realizes his error, he had not thought that they would still be watching as he left the safety of the alley but now four are following him. Muttering to himself, "feet don't fail me now", he runs full out, wanting for all the world to be as far from this place as he can be. He hears the call for him to stop, feels a wave of heat as a wand blast goes past his shoulder and he desperately dodges around a corner. His stomach spasms out of control as he sees the street is a dead end, devoid of any escape or cover to hide in. Coming to a stop he raises both his hands high in the air, turning in surrender and pleading, "Please stop! I mean you no harm! I am not your foe, have mercy!"

There are four of them two men both with swords drawn, the blond with the wand, and a robed woman who seems to glide up to him. The woman reaches out takes hold of his wrists and places cuffs on him. In a cold voice she says, "Mistress will determine your fate spy, now come easily and you will be well treated at least until she has judged you."

Wincing at the pronouncement of his fate, Cyril finds himself being not too gently urged forward flanked by guards with weapons drawn and ready. "Easy now, I'm sure this is all just a minor mistake. If your Mistress is busy I'll be happy to return tomorrow and explain myself". Cyril did not think that his bargaining would work but he never expected to be totally ignored. His captors merely keep up a steady pace at a heightened state of readiness, taking him back to the same doorway. He is dragged into a largish darkened room with a conspicuous throne centered on a dais along the back wall. The handcuffs on his wrists are unceremoniously chained to the floor in front of the throne. Without a single word, only the incantation needed to lock the door his four captors leave the room

Slipping a lock pick from the cuff on his shirt it takes him less than a minute to free himself from the chains. Knowing the door that they had entered by has been magically locked and that the exit his captors had taken was probably a bad bet, he searches for and finds a third exit, a curtain covered doorway. He slips through the curtain in silence and climbs the circular stairs winding upwards. The stairs end in a short hallway and he is now faced by three doors in front of him. Hoping to find any other way out of his captor's lair, he randomly chooses the door in front of him, his nimble fingers and well used picks soon open the lock. He quietly steps inside and closes the door behind him before turning and confronting the four armed residents, all staring at him with angry faces from behind drawn weapons. He swears to himself and is sure he hears the echo of his own asshole slamming shut!

Mistress Copper standing not two feet away with whip drawn, glares angrily at Cyril and merely motions to the floor snarling, "You have two choices, one is dying ! Get on your knees, NOW boy!"

Dropping to the floor, looking up about to begin to beg, Cyril, is silenced by the back of a hand slapping him across his face. "Stay down, shut up, and bloody well wait for us or I'll skin you alive!" are the only other words Mistress commands to the thief.

I can feel Mistress's turmoil, the controlled rage towards the intruder on the floor and how that rage is rapidly replaced with the same intensity by her caring for Sugar. Mistress goes to Sugar, cradles her gently and croons even though it is obvious to all that Sugar is only semi-conscious. I feel Mistress's care, her horror and worry, her pain and even her guilt is a palpable thing to me.

When Hex returns, she carries an ancient tome and a curious old scroll that she shows to Mistress and whispers in her ear. It is then that I feel the first glimmerings of relief from Mistress who nods saying, "Sugar must sleep now. Toy stay with her in case she wakes and is in need of anything." Turning to us, "Now let's go find out about this mystery man. He will be of use to us one way or another. So let's find out how."

Looking at the man, I see that he is more like a boy; he looks so scared he may even be rash enough to try to beg Mistress for mercy. I know that if he disturbs Sugar in any way Mistress will see him as an enemy. Taking pity on him I go over and grasp him by the ear, pulling him back through the door. Taken looking perplexed follows me closely as I drag him back down to where he had been chained. He comes easily for me, offering no resistance at all, but knowing Mistress and Hex also follow us down the stairs, I feel compelled to be perhaps rougher than I normally would. Still I make sure he does not actually fall or damage himself.

As Taken and I bring him to the floor below I nod to Taken and glance at the cupboards with a grin. I can feel Mistress's belief that unless something goes horribly wrong, this scrawny thief will at least contribute to our store of sperm potions. Knowing that Mistress will want him on his knees in front of her throne, I take him there and see the open cuffs still chained to the floor. I am not sure how he got out of them but leave all that to Mistress as I force him down on his knees.

Mistress seats herself on her throne, glaring at the lad before in a deadly soft voice asks, "What brings you to us boy? What manner of mischief rules this night?"

I can feel that Mistress is more curious than angry now, and hope she stays that way as I find this young man to be actually quite appealing. Even more so when he explains, "I was merely trying to find out what Sugar wanted with me. I had been told by more than a few people that she was looking for me. I was only coming to find out why when that attack happened. When I spotted the demon I just hid and did not offer assistance because I did not know what was happening. And well, I really don't think I could have done anything anyway." His voice just peters out under the silent stare of Mistress.

Gazing at him with interest a smile starting to lift the corner of her mouth, Mistress finally snorts in amusement saying, "Oh you're the one! You see my boy, I had actually asked Sugar to bring you home for a supper or a party." Mistress starts to laugh, and with a very pronounced wink says, "Pepper why don't you have Crap help you chain our thieving guest to your strongest table on wheels then bring him back to us covered in food, treats and condiments. For the life of me I can see no reason why we can't have that supper and a party while Sugar rests."

Taking a strange red and black device from her belt Mistress continues this time letting rage creep back into her voice. "I need to let Spite know what has happened. Deal with him! I have to call my First Girl."

Chapter Two

Macey opens her eyes, the coppery taste of blood still heavy on her palette. Naked, lying behind a rock she waits as her pounding heart gradually slows. She has landed hard in hell once more. Having your body destroyed in London is bad enough but to arrive back in hell naked and without weapons seems to be as much of an insult as being killed by mere mortals. The sky blue of her skin has faded back to its normal pale white shade; for only in London does her skin reflect the strength of her morality. But in looking down at her unclothed state the rage she feels inside, the burning bubbling disgust left over from the 'Seduction spell', the rage at being thrown naked, back into hell overwhelms her.

Jumping on the rock, stretching out her mouth and throat beyond what any human could attempt, she howls out hellfire. She screams the name of the mortal slut who must feel her wrath. The word starts with a low note that rapidly rises in pitch then dramatically falls back into a drawn out lower wail. 'Taken'! Is the only word that splits the stinking sulfuric air. Naked and weaponless, with the black blood rushing through her veins now tainted with hatred and disgust, every sense driven to the highest of alertness, she hears footsteps trying to creep closer to her.

She inhales deeply and catches the fetid stink of some near human creatures that attack the defenseless, even here. It would be too easy to just scare them away when ripping, rending and tearing would feel so much better.

15

Snarling, turning and leaping weaponless into a fray of her own making, she surprises seven of the scum, then with a blood stopping laugh, tears into them. Grabbing the first two by their throats she rips half of their necks away as she uses her cloven hoof to kick back into a charging foe's forehead, pounding it into a bloody pulp. With three dead or almost dead, the other four attackers stupidly close in, each trying to strike her with their pitifully inadequate weapons. Grinning, she spins and dodges while ripping them apart. A pirouette lets her slash with all ten of deadly talons, slashing at faces, throats and bellies with maniacal fury. Her long tail lashes out to skewer the last ugly still on his feet, right through its navel. Reveling in her attackers' pains, her own rage and the sheer glory of destruction, she drags the intestines out of the last one wraps it around his throat before bodily whirling the carcass and throwing it away.

Barely panting, more from rage than exertion she growls out her satisfaction, knowing full well that her rage has not even begun to be satiated. That would only come when she carves through the ribs and rips out the heart from her new target, the one called Copper's Taken.

With not even a backward glance she starts off for home, fully aware that true demons will be far more trouble and even less forgiving than those half creatures. She has to take care, not that she believes another demon on this plane would dare to attack her but rather to avoid knowledge of her defeat becoming known. Having her shame known by other Inquisitor demons would not result in a physical confrontation on the contrary she would only be shamed and placed in debt to whoever found her.

To avoid discovery, she takes a route that is far from direct, and travels the solitary path. Yet again, Macey did the one thing that she had hoped not to have to do ever again, slinking home, head hanging, tail tucked between her legs, doing the 'walk of shame'.

XXX

I am elsewhere in hell on a plane quite removed from the dismal caverns of Niffelem. Mistress had recently summoned me as her 'First Girl' Copper's Spite but I had returned after the business there was completed and have since spent several days chasing the one I had thrown down into hell. He had tried to kidnap my sister and paid for that with not only his life but his soul and freedom as well. It was in that last instant before he died his mortal's death, that he had given me his submission. He is a newly formed demon now but very weak. Somehow the sniveling wretch has been eluding me for several days. It is not really his fault that every time he is killed here he is thrown to another plane. The half men in hell are more numerous and dangerous that the ones in London. I have been forced to track him from one plane to the next. As near as I can tell he has been killed about eighteen times already. He is weak, weaponless, lost and probably in such a state of panic he cannot even figure out how to fight. But here in the Abyss I know he is closer than before, I can almost feel him or perhaps it is merely the enticing aroma that my sister Doll and I had left on him, I now know he is very close. He has to be afraid, the predators in hell are visibly much more gruesome than anything London can offer but those are only the first of his worries, he still carries the rank odor of hypocrisy on him. The stink of the Inquisitor in this plane of hell that is a defined Succi territory is such that if he were to meet any other demon here he would at best be attacked on sight or at worst have his newly formed submission snatched away from me.

Finding a sheltered spot where the renegade sub humans will not readily locate me, I sit cross legged and close my eyes, blocking out any and all interruptions. I follow the protocols of 'seeking' to take away all distractions before stretching out with my awareness, searching for the trace of my quarry's spore. With my mind and senses drifting free I can feel the trail. Rising up and standing, eyes still closed I can almost reach out my mind's hand towards him. There's the touch! I have him now! I know where he is as my mental fingers just barely brush against his mind. Grinning, I know he is in a state of total panic. He did not feel my probe; I know that just as I am aware he does not know how or why he keeps coming back to life after being repeatedly ripped apart. Opening my eyelids, not needing the probe again I stride off in his direction. As I stalk him I also double check the contents of my war pack anticipating his capture. It takes a while but every minute is worth it, the anticipation seems to make the time spent stalking him endless. Finally surreptitiously I arrive in the area where he is hiding. Peering around in the forest I locate him hiding behind some rocks and vegetation. His fear is a palpable scent now, one that is attracting some very nasty undead. I know he has no hope to survive against those foes and that if they kill him he will once again be thrown to a different plane, if that happens I'll have to start all over again. Well that is not going to happening! I have had just about enough of this hide and seek shit! I growl just deep enough in my throat to attract the attention of the undead and as they turn to face me, I let my rage bloom like a frightful flower. My leap to a mortal would be super human but here I merely land effortlessly trident in hand. A single spinning attack kills one and cripples a second, leaving me standing with my back to the third. Predictably the monster attacks my exposed back, laughing I stab back under my arm with the single spike at the butt end of my trident, ripping up under the creature's jaw almost severing its head. Now I am on top of this situation at last, the very thought of having finally found my new slave has turned me almost giddy. I purposefully stride to the rocky hiding place of my cowering slave and grab him by his hair dragging him out into the open.

"You are MINE! Damn you! You have been hiding from me! That will stop now and forever, understood?" My words are intoned with the same brutality as the body slams I am giving him as I repeatedly throw him down. His reply, if there ever was one is gone with the air that is forced from his lungs. I drive the very last of the air he breathes from his chest as I land on his battered form with both knees on his lower shoulder blades. Pressing down hard my full weight on my knees, I grab his hair pulling his head back, finally giving me the long awaited chance to clamp and lock my collar around his gasping throat. Licking his cheek with my split tongue I murmur, "You're MINE now and you are going to need some serious training Boyo, so the sooner we start the better."

Standing I snap a leash on the collar's hasp and grab the gasping demon's arms, dragging them behind his back and painfully chaining his elbows together. I feel elated I have him! The very first slave I have ever thrown down to hell. I may be Mistress Copper's First Girl which generally puts me in charge of all those she called MINE, but I have never really owned another slave's leash before. I have helped enslave and train many but never one that was mine, all mine!

Knowing full well that my chain work will hold him fast, I delight for a minute in just to watching him. I should actually now give him a token reward, I must become his first, last and only hope. Cooing softly into his ear I say, "You are going to come with me now Boyo I'm taking you home with me, to make you into a good little slave boy!"

Whining in fear he begs, "Please Mistress, I could not find you."

What shit is this? I whirl around grabbing his hair, shaking and slapping him hard enough to all but rattle his teeth lose , sputtering in rage, "You whiney worm, you dare to refer to yourself as an 'I' in front of me? I own your ass! You're my PROPERTY! Property does not say I! I'm taking you home now, where I'll whip that whining ass, **which I own**, into a bloody pulp!" Then in an only partially acted rage I drag him to his feet, tightly clenching his collar in my fist and casting the spell that takes us both back to my home plane of Pandemonium.

Still angry, I cannot help but congratulate myself with a nod of approval at my landing spot, very nearly next door to my front doors. This is about the most perfectly placed landing site I could have asked for. Forcing my new slave ahead of me, giving him not a moment to rest or even have a chance of getting his bearings, I bodily force him through the double doors of my mansion. Taking him by a short leash I brutally drag him behind me, going through numerous hidden doors to descend several floors into the dankest part of my home. Having reached the dungeon, I force my slave's face to the floor where I lock the collar to a ring firmly embedded there.

"You were making me very angry and your first lesson will be to learn just how bad a thing that is." I say with a sadistic smile to my now silent demon slave, "But I have you and your whiney mouth back now just in time to start your training as my slave. Those near creatures that kept killing you are something you don't have to worry about any more now that you're my slave, I shall protect you from everything."

He needs to see me as at least partly as a sadistically all seeing force, far above and beyond him. So with a glance down I walk behind him and begin by dragging the sharpened tines of my trident down his upper back. Reveling in the pain I am causing, I smile and grin maliciously as I slice skin and flesh to the bone, pressing the trident down until I see the white of his ribs showing through the torn flesh. I take great care as I create three jagged edged wounds that run down his back, the center one on his spine, the other two running parallel. With my voice deliberately contrived as cold, callous and flat I begin by questioning him, "Do you like the pain slave?"

Not even waiting for an answer I continue, "Is it intense enough to get your attention? You shall learn that each and every time you utter any word like 'I', or 'me' the pain will only get worse." To emphasis, my meaning, I scream "FAR, FAR WORSE!"

Following the loud shout with a gentle sound, I whisper softly, "But you are just not going to say those words are you? You are going to learn to be a good slave." I tap my hoof in front of his face to emphasize my question. "You are not going to say those words, WHY? I will tell you the reason only once. The reason is that you will give up and forever renounce being anything but my property! You will learn that the greatest thing in your life is to please me because failure is eternal torment."

Pressing my hoof into his cheek I continue speaking in a more even tone. "Before I owned you there was a name that belonged to you. Now I own you and whatever that name was, it is now gone! I prefer another name. From now on and for all eternity your name will be 'Spite's Boyo'." Smiling I lean down and draw the talons on my index finger along the bleeding furrow running down Boyo's back before licking it with my forked tongue to taste his blood. "Mmmm, you do taste delightful but I do not think I have heard your reply, slave?"

"Yes Mistress. Your slave, Spite's Boyo will not say those words ever again. Your slave thanks you for allowing him to have a name chosen by you Mistress."

As I look down at Boyo I can almost pity him. He was a few short days ago a free mortal but he had been captured and with Doll's help had his very soul sacrificed. That sacrifice had gone so well that at the very end of his life he had acknowledged me as his Mistress. Now after finding out just how hellish hell can be, he has convincingly reaffirmed his submission. I know from his response that he has seen enough slaves to know full well what is expected of him, as well as how far from a free Inquisitor Adept he has fallen. All I have to do now is emphasize his condition before rewarding him beyond any poor Inquisitor imaginings.

"You are new here in hell. You have not learned what eternal torment is all about." I say this as I carefully and very gently run one of the trident tines over the ball of his hoof. He needs to have everything I have said emphasized in an extreme manner so I do what must be done and I lean my whole weight on the trident forcing the center tine through the ball of his hoof and into the stone floor. As my new boy slave screams in agony, I merely ignore his pleadings to be released from the pain. "Mistress please your slave will obey and worship you but please, please give him your sweet mercy."

I stare into his eyes, my face set in a cold sneer, "If you were so foolish as to displease me, you do not deserve my mercy. I can keep you screaming for all eternity and increase the pain every hour. Think for a second of that old Greek legend where the God's chained the immortal one who gave man fire to a mountain top just so that every day the eagles could rips his liver out. I want you to remember that legend and remember that I don't need to find a mountain top to chain you to and that I can cause far more pain than any old liver loving eagle."

After connecting the chain between his elbows to another hanging from a ceiling pulley, I yank hard pulling him up against his impaled hoof and his chained throat. Bending over to whisper into his ear, "Now Boyo, say the words I need to hear, speak to me of your only desire."

My slave shudders, moaning in agony, his eyes droop in defeat, even his voice is now tired worn and pleading, "Please Mistress, let your slave serve you."

I have to show him the satisfaction he has brought me. I smile the smile that Mistress has said lights my face. Pulling my trident from his hoof I carefully place it in a rack on the wall before releasing his collar from the ring on the floor. "You have only started to learn Boyo but I think with just a bit more encouragement you will be totally MINE." To emphasize my words I once again drag hard on the chain hanging from the ceiling, raising him up by the bindings between his elbows until he is almost on tip toes. With his upper body bent slightly forward he tries to raise his head only to encounter my pierced and chained nipple directly in front of his mouth. Glancing up in confusion he sees me grin at him then step back and go to the same rack that now holds my trident, taking out a short switch.

I deliberately speak in happy but conversational tones, almost as if it was the most normal thing in the world to have a demon slave bound almost suspended in my dungeon. Turning to him, "Not now Boyo, perhaps later we will play but there are a few little lessons you must learn first." Striding back behind my slave I lash out with the switch striking low on his buttocks. "You first need to learn to pay attention." Proceeding by crossing the red welt from my first strike with one that follows the crack of his ass, I continue, "You have to know, really know, that your whole existence must be solely rooted in pleasing me and me alone. Do you understand slave?"

Boyo gasps rapidly, "Yes Mistress, oh yes Mistress! Your least wish is this slave's command!"

Toying with Boyo to make sure he will remember, I use the switch to slash another welt parallel to the first creating the capital letter I. "That was not a bad response slave but I'd like to hear more begging in your voice. Are you going to really beg me slave?"

"Yes Mistress! Please Mistress! Your slave begs to obey only you! Please let this slave serve you in anyway, at any time in any place!"

Reaching out I release the chain dropping him back to the cold stone floor and with a word and a gesture I heal his wounds leaving only painless marks. My new slave goes to his knees, placing his head directly in front of my hooves saying fervently with relief, "Your Boyo thanks you Mistress, your spell is very welcome."

I place the switch on the floor in front of him, instructing, "Now my Boyo use your lips, not your teeth and pick up my switch and place it on the weapons rack then get your mangy ass back here!"

Crawling forward, pressing his lips over the switch handle, tasting the stone grit from the floor, he carefully lifts the switch and struggles to climb to his hooves. Slipping backwards once, he presses his lips together hard not wanting to drop the whip. But finally gaining his balance he walks over to the wall and with the greatest of care places the switch on a tray of the rack. But his replacing of the switch is hardly the point I wanted to make. I want him to sneak a peek into the tray which also contains a riding crop, a collar with spikes facing inwards, a coiled bull whip, several small very sharp looking knives, a decidedly oversized butt plug and even a sharpened spoon with a series of clamps. Equally daunting are three dildos: one strap on version about the size of a normal man's member carved out of wood but studded with brass knobs. The second an ass spreader, also of wood has three separate parts, two long pieces connected by a cord at one end, with a wedge shaped third piece that slides inside separating the other two pieces. But the third toy is the most daunting, it has the same sort of handle as a sword complete with a hilt but beyond the hilt is a good foot and a half long solid iron dildo at least four inches in diameter. These three items lay strewn among several brightly colored silken strips of cloth. After shuddering at the sight of these objects and at a variety of different whips and switches hanging on the outside of the rack he carefully makes his way back to his Mistress where he kneels, eyes to the floor in fear and awe.

"Did you see something you liked in my toy tray?" I ask deliberately, and then wait in expectation of his answer.

"Mistress your slave has not used items like this before so cannot say, but trusts you to teach him."

"Oh yes I shall, but later I think." I reach out patting his head, pausing briefly to stroke his horns before leaning forward and whispering, "Now that was not so bad was it Boyo?" Not waiting for a reply I continue, "You have started to be a good slave, so now you are going to be rewarded with the opportunity to please me."

After slipping off my body armor I wrap one of my hard muscled thighs over his shoulder and with a forward thrust of my hips, I press myself into his waiting face. I know how well he has responded to the arousal my pheromones naturally create but that was as a mortal in London, that time I took his very life and soul back with me to hell. Now I need more, I need my Demonic Succi's lust incarnate to bring me his undead devotion.

I have surrounded his face; he has no option but to deeply drink of my arousing aroma. Granting him a bit of time to let himself become enthralled once more, I sigh deeply when his tongue licks up between my lips before kissing and sucking on my clit. Shuddering I take him by one horn and the hair at the back of his head and press his face harder into me. "Ah now there is a tongue as well as lips that hold the promise of delight. But you will have to really use it if you expect to please me Boyo." Guiding him back and down to the cold stone floor, I kneel straddling his head while pulling up on his horns to place his mouth just where I need it. As I grind my hips into him I can feel the bubbling rush of pure arousal well up, flooding his face with my juices. The satisfaction of having him so totally in my control is going to continue to make this a great cumming. This slave is MINE, all mine and I'm going to make him perfect.

I could let myself go on and on, but I stop, control must now be exercised properly. I slither back down his body, over and past his erect member until I can press both of my breasts on either side of his cock. I hear him groan again this time not in pain as I slowly move my sweat slicked ample globes up and down over his trapped cock. Sliding my hips down far enough for his cloven hoof to tease my clit, I flick my forked tongue over his meat like a little lash. Looking up at him I see his mouth is slightly open with his eyes closed in complete absorption. Choosing that minute, I raise my ass from his hoof, I rub the tip of my tail over my wetness, curling it down, I caress his hole with this sharp tip before pressing and forcing up and in with the wide end of my tail. His mouth and eyes fly open as his ass is breached; I can feel how his ass spasms and contracts as he grips my tail hard. I keep on pressing in and pulling out harder and faster. With every stroke of my tongue on his cock now timed to the thrust of my tail, I settle myself back onto his hoof just in time to feel it curl and twitch. Wiggling myself down it easily enters me and I feel the mounting of my own burning response. The way the sweat on his forehead is beading, the way he is now looking at me and the way I feel his body strung as taught as a bow string shows me the precise instant to reward both of us.

I take hold of his balls and give a sharp tug saying, "Not quite yet Boyo you're going to have to keep it inside a bit longer than that." With these words, I lower myself onto his rigid cock and rock my hips from side to side loving the way his rampant rod fills me completely. Thrusting up and down on him I lean back stretching myself over him as I guide his cock onto my passion place and clamp myself around his cock. At last with my head rolling back on my shoulders I grind myself into his pelvis.

We both erupt together, him crying out, "Mistress!"

I at the peak of my passion, howl out, "MINE!"

Briefly falling forward to hold him tight I look into his eyes seeing only surrender as I lick my lips before standing over him. He now looks as completely spent as I feel invigorated. I grab his hair once more and drag his unresisting body to a slave pen, pushing him in, locking it up before taking him some demon meat. I had planned to just sit and watch him eating while mentioning some of those things he has to fear in hell and why he needs to stay in his cage. But changing my mind, I go to the weapon rack and take out a my twelve foot razor weighted war whip, just to reinforce the idea that there is less of a need to fear what was outside my doors and more of a need to fear me. Cracking the whip just at the edge of the bars of the slave pen, I merely explain, "You are safe inside that pen, outside you will learn more of pain than you ever dreamed existed, so sit and stay!"

Turning to leave, I am surprised when my red and black hell-phone's ringer goes off. The familiar Gregorian chant draws my attention away from my slave as only one other, Mistress Copper, knows of this number. Taking it out, I make a mental note to get Boyo his own hell-phone just in case he manages to wander off in the future.

The tone I hear in Mistress's voice shocks me enough to know that I have to get out of my slave's sight, now! Something very bad has happened so even before responding, I dash to the stairs. Mistress's voice erupts from the phone, dripping rage and violence.

"That hell-blue bitch Macey attacked us, she critically injured my Sugar," were the first words yelled. They bring me to an abrupt halt. With these words I feel my lips pull back revealing my fangs and my tail whipping from side to side in anger. Sugar is more than just my sister; we have done so many things together. In that part of my life, I had before being sent to hell she had been my sole companion. Not everything we had done was nice but she had always stood back to back with me when there was a need. An injury to her was also an insult to me. An insult I would not tolerate!

"How badly is Sugar hurt? Can't she be healed? How will your First Girl avenge this Mistress?"

Mistress let's acid drip from her tongue, but it does not reassure me. "My sweet Sugar can barely speak; her throat is so badly damaged. We healed her fast enough for her to live but the five scars from that blue bitch's talons go so deep that they have ruined her voice. My Hex found an old and long forgotten scroll that contains a cure. However, that cure indicates that we will have to take her on a quest to remove the scars. As to your request you do not attack today. I know you are angry, I can feel your rage all the way from hell but all you are going to do today is gather some friends who will attack that bitch tomorrow and each day after that. I don't want her able to be summoned until I have had the time for a proper trap to be set. That will be your job, keeping her in hell until I'm ready for her. Do you understand MINE?"

There was no choice here Mistress had seen to that. I had explicit orders and they would be obeyed to the letter. My trained response pops out of my mouth as if it has been planning its escape for months, "Yes Mistress!"

I want to go rend and destroy now! But I know, even as Mistress breaks the connection, this is not the way Mistress has planned it, so it will not happen. I will go, my rage controlled to look up a few old friends. I dress in my armor and leave the house without a backward glance. I snarl as I walk.

Chapter Three

Mistress Copper snarls and slips her hellphone back onto her belt while listening to the fading protestations of the panicky thief that can barely be heard as he is dragged off to the kitchen by a laughing pair of her slaves. "No, there's been a mistake!"

Taking a deep breath Mistress turns motioning Cum to her side saying, "Cum I have an important errand for you. I want you to go to HFC and bear my invitation to Dovey. I want her to come to a most interesting supper."

Turning to her 'Hire Sword', Slice, "Could you accompany Cum please? I'd really like your sister Dovey to join us and I don't feel all that comfortable about sending out any of MINE alone after what has just happened to Sugar." Looking around once more to Hex, "You should go as well just in case they need a bit of magic to back them up. When the lot of you get there, it will be easier for all of you to convince her that Pepper is doing something special but keep the details a surprise. Dovey loves Pepper's cooking almost as much as Pepper loves Dovey's compliments."

After making a shooing gesture to the trio she turns to Taken and I and says, "I need to talk to you two before things get even more out of control. Doll, your sister Hex made two observations that were unexpected. First, she observed your shot that killed the stupid bird. That kill has been tried unsuccessfully a thousand times before, those damned things have been spying on everyone in London for years, nobody knows why they do it but many have tried to find out. You are the very first to actually have your shot strike home. She paid you the highest of compliments saying you did not fire your wand but rather your awareness made your weapon fire. I'm not sure what that even means but from her it is high praise. The second was what she found in the carcass of that bird some small bit of gold and ceramic possibly some magically electronic hybrid device but very much beyond anything we have here, so things are strange to the extreme!"

Turning to my sister she continues, "Taken you by all reports fought well. Moreover, you had the uncommon good sense to find out what the whole attack was about. This is a very good thing my dear and I do congratulate you. You are making me proud already love. But the bad news is the reason that the blue demoness came, that blue hellion was summoned to specifically attack my Doll, so war is upon us! I'm afraid my dear that while Doll was her first target, the way you defeated Macey will make you her target of choice. My enemy Malthus is her brother, he will summon her back just as soon as he can. It is only a matter of time before he brings her back to London again. But this time she is going to be confused for now when she is brought back, she will have two targets not one. I know Spite will do her best, I know she will hound that hellion from plane to plane to plane but she needs to kill her daily to prevent a successful summoning. So it is only a matter of timing before Malthus summons her prior to Spite killing her that day. She will be back on our doorstep and she will then hunt with a vengeance. He will insist she go after Doll all over again; she will want to go after you. She will have to make a choice between you and Doll. We must hope indecision will be her undoing, if you see that confusion strike first and strike to kill! It may well be your only hope. Now come with me MINE! We must see to Sugar."

XXX

Meanwhile, I, Cyril, now left alone in the kitchen with the slave called Pepper after Crap had left; look up in askance at her.   They had pointedly and totally ignored any and all of my protestations even though I was using some of my very best lines. Pepper and her sister stripped and chained me naked to a two foot high table on wheels. It was not as if they were being harsh or cruel, the way they were laughing I had to think this must be some sort of joke, even if the joke is on me it hasn't hurt me yet. They had taken great care to tightly chain me with both my arms and legs stretched open and away from my body immobile. It was then with a wink that the other slave girl had left me alone with Pepper. I had been taught all about locks by a pretty market thief who had come and gone, probably to jail but I could see no way to defeat these locks. I have no choice but to lay there and hope I can enjoy myself.

She is very pretty dressed in little more than an apron, collar and chains. Her skin is a sort of a dusky color that almost glows in the light of the overhead window but her crowning glory is her cascading curls of reddish hair.   She looks amused and really quite pleased with herself. Actually her smile is the one thing helping me to keep all this in perspective and she is a great perspective. I'm chained to a table that is fully 8 feet long by three feet wide with no way to get free and even less of an idea of what is going to happen to me but I am under the impression that this will not be all that bad.

Trying yet again I suggest, "You are very lovely. I would really like to spend some time with you but really these chains are just not needed. You and I could have a wonderful time together. Do you know I bet we would both enjoy it so much better without these silly chains?" Continuing to look up at her even though I really don't have a lot of choice, it is not hard to see that she is only amused at what I have to say. But there is more than amusement in those eyes and that grin, she appears curious about something but let's face it at least she is not mad at me. I can tell she has thoroughly looked me over and is not in the least embarrassed by my nudity; rather her attention is drawn by my tattoos. The look of wonder written across her face is enticing in itself; I can feel myself starting to harden. She lets her hands drop to my chest and starts to trace parts of the tattoo with her figertips. It is like a sweet torture! Her gentle touch serves to make me test the chains that I know are unbreakable, if only I could take her in my arms! Her fingers delicately trace through the intricate ink work that depicts Doves, dead and alive as well as the reds, whites and greens of flowers and vines, also dead and alive, until finally she traces the words stained into my upper chest 'Love Over all.' I gasp at her touch, squeezing my eyes shut, caught unable to touch her but needing her touch so badly.

I hear her voice come to me, almost in an awed whisper. "However did you ever get that tattoo done?" She asked in all honesty. I really wanted to tell her some exotic fable but as her fingers dropped to play with my pubic hairs I can only gulp and sheepishly admit.

"I had only been in London for couple of days and was drinking up some found money. I sort of remember a girl who took me home, but the next thing I do remember was waking up like this almost twelve hours later with the worst hangover and draped over a porcelain throne."

Gratefully she ends my babbling by gently placing her fingers across my lips and kissing my cheek. At first gently letting the tip of her tongue just barely touch my skin then with more vigor as she brushes her lips over mine and our breaths merge with mouths drawn closer together, appreciating each and every scrap of contact between the sensitive skins of each other's lips. Drawing back once more she holds her finger over my lips saying, "Shhhh, you are not going to be harmed but you will provide Mistress with a lot of amusement."

She continues almost solemnly, "You may not know how close to dying you actually came today. The last person whose behavior towards one of Mistress Copper's house was thought to be offensive, found himself fucked to death then dragged down to hell as a slave. Now that did not happen to you even better you are not screaming in pain, so if you stop and think for just a minute, you may realize that if you co-operate and if you are even just a little bit lucky, you just might get out of this with not only your hide intact but well and truly laid to boot." Grinning Pepper reaches down and teases my belly and pubic hairs, "But for now you are all mine and let this slave assure you that she is not even going to start to harm you."

While I was not really enthralled to hear about what had happened to the last person that pissed off this slave's Mistress, it certainly takes the edge off to hear that I may actually have a really good time instead, so I just close my mind to that and comfort myself by gazing up at the Lovely in front of me. Her white apron covers her from above her full breasts down to just above her knees and peeking out under the apron is a gold silken sash around her hips. There is also a copper colored collar etched with the words, 'Copper's Pepper' encircling her beautiful neck with some fine chains hanging down from it, ending somewhere under her apron as well as copper wrist and ankle cuffs. Her grin is almost as contagious and arousing as her teasing of my belly and groin, that is until she turns from me to a screeching kettle displaying one of the juiciest looking asses I have yet seen. From the angle of my prone perch I can just see her taking out some towels and pouring the boiling water over them, which also affords me a great view of her ass and legs as they bend, tighten and then straighten to replace the kettle. What a feast for the eyes, if this girl can cook up something even half as tasty as this vision is she may well be the one of the greatest chefs in London. I have her pleasantly fixed in my fantasies right up to the point where she carefully carries over the pot holding the towels and begins to sharpen a glinting one edged blade on a long leather strop. "Uhh, what are you doing with those?" I almost stutter in confusion. Trying to divert the girl back to my more pleasurable ideas, "You do know that if you were to unchain me we really could have a wonderful time here?"

Grinning and using tongs, Pepper takes out a steamy towel and lets it drain for a minute. She goes on to say, "I'm going to give you a little shave now. I would never serve food off of a platter that is not completely spotless and I'm not going to start with you either. That lovely blonde hair on your head is so heavenly that I could never take that from you, I'll just have to do something else with it but the rest of your hair is going to be gone, every single whispering whisker of it. I can personally not think of a better way to clean you up than to give you a full body shave."

I try to explain that a nice hot bath with her would have the same effect but her lips stop mine in a protracted kiss followed by a lewd and lascivious giggle. She stifles my logical retort by wrapping steamy hot towel over my face and saying, "Enjoy! Most people would pay a fortune to have this done by me!" The shock of the screaming heat hitting my face takes my breath away. I cannot even see as my eyes are also covered but I can hear her using a brush to whip the soap into lather. But the heat is totally negated by the cool air as she peals away the towel and replaces it into the pot. Now she merely flourishes the brush with confidence and skill spreading the foamy solution over my cheeks, chin and throat. With style and panache, Pepper skillfully wields that honed blade and carefully exfoliates my face. It is actually comforting as the edge passes over the base of my throat easily slicing through any bit of beard that had been there. Now I have every trust that this lovely slave is fully competent to give the closest and cleanest of shaves. Smiling down at me after this treat Pepper croons, "Now was that so bad? Not even the tiniest nick." Finishing by spreading a fragrant cream over my face she adds, "When was the last time you had such a pleasant shave? Are you ready for more?"

She proceeds to gingerly take up the steamy hot towel once again this time plastering it over the tattoos on my chest. The further Pepper proceeds, the greater the confidence I feel until her sheering strokes and the gentle scrapings begin to actually start to arouse me. In this manner Pepper moves down from my shoulders and chest all the way to my hips. I had not been overly aroused before but now my near rigid cock is like a mast proclaiming to all of the dusky slave's skill, not surprisingly the lower she goes the higher my cock rises. After reaching my hips she continues down my legs leaving only my thighs and groin and my flagpole unshaved.

Pepper leers at me before she oh so sweetly blows me a little kiss. My sighs of pleasure of her shaving me must tell her just how wonderful this feels. I am so comfortable with her ministrations that I relax into near bliss until she sets down the razor and tugs one my toes, examining it and clucking at what she sees. Pursing her lips she examines each toe and nail in turn before turning to me and saying, "What a dreadful state of affairs. Your feet and nails have been sadly neglected. These will have to be done properly before I can ever think of serving food on you." Taking two of the steamy towels she wraps each foot then lifts out the last towel and moves to spread it over my groin.

I'm sure my eyes jump out of my head, as the heat from the towel toasts my most tender flesh. I can hardly even speak; only sort of whimper, "Take that off, for the sake of all that is Holy! Please, take that off! It's burning the balls off me!" That hot towel was like a cold shower that causes my cock to drop in response.

Pepper that beautiful cruel temptress just shakes her head and giggles before returning to strop the razor once more saying as she does, "Oh quiet there my fine tattooed friend in just a minute your cock will have my razor on it but do you realize that after your shaving is complete you are going to have a full pedicure? I simply cannot let those nails interfere with the presentation of my feast." Looking around her she continues, "You know if this slave had not already completed most of the food preparations she would be quite annoyed at you. She just hates to be interrupted especially when she cooks but as it is everything is under control." With a smirk she turns away saying, "And you should be very glad about that." Reaching out and stroking down my now smooth belly to the towel hiding the short and curlies at my groin. She moves her lips to my ear and whispers, "I may even have enough time for us to get all hot and bothered before I start to dress you."

First flourishing the tongs and then tearing the towel from me, with a cheerful smile she lathers my cock and balls. Chained or not, this time I have far more sense than to dare to try to pull back or fruitlessly fight the chains. Looking up at her calm expression I can imagine her looking at a live bird in exactly the same way just before she cuts off its head and I have some head I really, really do not want cut off. I freeze in place as her fingers pull and stretch my skin, just before that first initial steely contact.

I look up at her and have to beg, "You don't want to get blood all over so why don't we just pretend that you have finished?" But after seeing her giggling I realize that the better part of valor may be to not distract her, so I just close my eyes saying, "No I suppose you are going to do exactly what you intend to do, no matter what I say or do" and she does.

Feeling her fingers take hold of the folds of lose skin below my cock, I shudder and fix my eyes at a very interesting knot in the wood of a beam above us as she stretches tight the skin and begins to scrape the edge again and again over my bag. My jaw starts to ache because my teeth are so tightly clenched. I feel the panic involuntarily rise in me as I lay there chained, bound and controlled while every last hair is shaved from my body. But wonder of wonders, somehow all of me has survived intact! Looking up I have to bless the skills of this lovely slave as there is not so much as a nick anywhere on me. I close my eyes in relief and let the last of the pent up air escape from my lungs but I only just have time to inhale deeply before feeling a new attack on my manhood. When I feel the slave Pepper's moist lips kiss the very tip of my cock, my eyes fly open in sheer amazement. For with a lick of her lips and a flick of her hips, Pepper drops both her apron and her sash to the floor and looks over at me with doe like eyes.

Chained in place I want to reach out and hold her but can only strain at my bindings. Looking at her I see once again just how beautiful she is, her smoky skin and fiery hair glistening in the light cascading through a high window, her nipples on perky breasts pierced and chained, her eyes so alive and inviting. I know that my chains would be easier to break free from than this vision. Her nails draw thin white lines across my belly and chest, moaning in response to this scratching that demands my attention, I can only writhe and twitch to her touch. Her tongue strokes down my cock from tip to base, I just can't help my hips from bucking up as my body's shudder signifies my reactions to the contrast between the scratching nails and enticing tongue. But when she covers the helm of my cock with her lips I have a treat I have not experienced before. My skin so recently shaved is alive like never before, feeling everything with an intensity that is completely new to me. First blowing down on my cock she sucks gently using her fingers and lips to bring my foreskin higher on my almost hard cock. Teasing her tongue between the foreskin and my helm she tantalizes me until I am so hard that the expanding shaft of my cock pulls the foreskin from her tongue. Now with a rampant erection I strain at the chains desperately tugging, trying hard just to touch or hold this vision of passion and bringing new meaning to the table's name of the groaning board. Pepper has started to move her whole head up and down over my cock as I feel myself turning into fleshy steel. I am just so aroused that I am trembling in the chains unable to do anything more than thrust with my hips and moan for more.

Pepper slowly crawls onto the groaning board and over my body, licking, scratching, nibbling, from my cock up to my lips finally kissing me deeply as she raises her hips easily sliding my cock deep into her while straddling my groin. Raising her head as she rocks back settling onto my cock so it slides deep inside, she closes her eyes digging her fingernails into my chest. Bending forward suddenly her tongue slips between my lips and teeth just as I thrust up forcing my cock deeper into her. Her tongue retreats from my mouth as her hips pull her off my cock, but both return, her hips to enfold me, her tongue to invade me, timed with pleasure and passion. Sitting up now rocking and rolling her hips with mine; her head rolls back on her shoulders as she moans softly. "Before this chef makes you into the best serving platter in London she has to make sure you know just how good it gets. Now don't you cum just yet my friend let's make sure that every single cell on your body is ready to be licked clean."

I am now so confused I feel my mind reeling. I am the one that steals kisses but now someone else is stealing my heart and I know it. "Oh Please, just be with me! You are so wonderful!" I try to beg and again, "Please don't let it end, you are so amazing I just want more!"

Pepper grins down and whispers, "Let me show you why Mistress gave me the name, Copper's Pepper Grinder." She rolls her hips in slow circles and grinds herself down on my cock timing her gyrations to the thrust of my hips, meeting, matching and joining ours every move. Pepper grinds and contracts around my cock her motions spiking both of us over the edge into mutual orgasms.

Bathed together in the bright sun from the skylight, we find ourselves bursting forth like the dawning of a new day. As she lies on top of me she says, "You see my sweet platter, when Mistress first made me one of those she calls MINE she had a little problem." Continuing with a smile and a giggle, "She wanted to call me Pepper because her new slave was so saucy but when she took me to bed she declared I was a grinder and that was why on my first collar this girl was named 'Copper's Pepper Grinder'. But that didn't work too well as most people found it too long, so later after this girl's cooking was up to the standards Mistress demanded, Mistress shortened the name to Copper's Pepper. This girl thinks Mistress might have done that because her slave is so very good at spicing everything up."

We both laugh at the history and she hugs and kisses me until a bell rings over a large oven. Getting up Pepper looks down at me saying, "It is almost time to start dressing you for dinner love; you are going to be the tastiest treat in all of London before I'm done with you. But first let's look at those feet." Rummaging in a drawer she takes out a file with a tapered end and a tiny pair of manicure scissors saying, "Toe time toots!"

Chapter Four

As Cum, Hex and Slice enter the Hell Fire Club, generally referred to as the HFC, they see the normally crowded bar has only a half a dozen patrons being served by eight statuesque slave girls. They are greeted not by the normal hustle and bustle of the bar but rather by an almost empty and greatly subdued scene. The spotlessly clean low slung couches and tables have only fractional use and even the near naked dancer seems to be somewhat uninspired. Dovey rising from a customer's side, looks up at her brother saying, "Slice, where have you been hiding? The last I saw of you, you were playing shepherd to Copper's girls and Cum? Not that I have had a lot happening here ever since that attack, the business has been tapering off badly." Then after a pregnant pause, "Almost as if people did not want to be out in the streets for fear of war or something."

Slice answers in feigned innocence's, "War, what war? I've just been a guest at Mistress Copper's. As a matter of fact, I was asked to accompany Cum and Hex while they bring you an invitation." His smile is so large and genuine that anyone seeing it would have to believe that the smile is either a joke or the gospel truth. Slice pushes Cum forward encouraging him to deliver the message and is amused at how he towers over his little sister.

Cum who would normally never desire to be the center of attention, looks more than a little embarrassed but somehow manages to not quite stammer out his greetings, "This slave has been charged to deliver an invitation from his Mistress, Mistress Copper, to you Silver Dove. The invitation is to attend tonight's special supper that Mistress personally guarantees will bring no end of pleasure for you. This slave is further charged that with the aid of my sister Hex and your noble brother Slice, we escort you back to Mistress's house." Then getting down on one knee and lowering his head he begs, "Please accept. Mistress was most insistent that you attend Ma'am."

Looking around her Dovey sighs, "Well if there ever was a good time to take a bit of time for myself, this might very well be it. I feel as if I have been cooped up in this bar for months and this is the first time that business has slacked off. Giselle come here girl." As a tall, lithe blond dancer comes over to her much shorter, stouter Mistress and kneels, Dovey continues, "I'm going out and may be gone all night or perhaps even more, Copper normally has a good reason for giving invitations to anything. You will be in charge while I am gone but I want you to remember that I will require a full accounting after I return."

The slave girl nods and rises, saying only, "Yes Mistress!"

As she leaves Slice playfully slaps the slave's shapely ass and winks at her, "I'll personally see to your accounting and work on your dancing as well later." He then bends down over his sister whispering something into her ear, as he uses his massive bulk to gently guide her out through the doorway.

Dovey eyes her brother as she feels his arm drape over her shoulder and whispers back, "REALLY? She said that? 'In like Sin'!" Dovey squeezes her knees and arms together proudly grinning while looking in admiration up at her brother.

The four emerge from the doorway of HFC into the warm late morning sun, Cum leading as he had been instructed, fully armored with shield on his arm and two blades resting in their scabbards, but immense as Cum is he is not quite dwarfed by the immensity of the near giant Slice. Those two hulking warriors both with the heavy weapons and armor are in startling contrast to Dovey who is far shorter than the norm. For Dovey who is garbed in a combination of armor and light flowing robes that unsuccessfully hide the fact that she is noticeably and decidedly rounder as well as shorter than the others. In the rear comes Hex who is yet another anomaly, thin, totally covered except for just the suggestion of a dark face beneath her cowled green and gold robe. She holds the same sort of wand as Dovey but longer and much more intricate. What sets her apart from everyone is the very way she moves; her feet are unseen beneath her robes, she does not appear to take steps, rather she seems to glide along the streets and through the underground. Together the four companions make their way back home to the house of Mistress Copper.

Taken and I stay at Mistress's throne curled like kittens around her feet and legs as she reads through several crackle dry parchment scrolls. I can't feel her in my mind except to understand she is concentrating hard on the translation of the very old, barely visible scripts. I know this has something to do with Sugar and she does not want to be disturbed. After gently touching Taken to get her attention, I place my finger on my lips to let her know Mistress must be left to her tasks and not disturbed.

I have learned from Mistress that my branding has somehow uniquely unleashed an ability to share the feelings and the sensations that she or I are experiencing, moreover if there is a single strongly held emotion or perception that too can be communicated. She has told me that it is not an unusual event for a branded slave to becomes more obedient to the commands of the one that pressed the red hot metal into her flesh but no one in Mistress's experience has had such a complete bonding as the one she has formed on me. What has happened between us is an extremely rare and unusual event. In the past Mistress has only heard references to this occurrence but has never actually seen or met anyone like us. She had been worried that I could be stolen far easier than another girl or even be seduced with greater ease but when she told Hex, the most powerful spell caster in her house to use a seduce spell on me, the spells failed consistently.

I have had little time to explore this idea that I am different from my brother and sisters but the closeness of the bonding between Mistress and me is so wonderful that I'm having trouble even imagining why anyone would not want the intimacy of our bond.

Even though Mistress does not hear the front door open, because I do, she raises her head in response. I feel her satisfaction at my alertness and smile up at her unspoken compliment. Rising to a ready position and pulling Taken with me, we go to stand guard beside the door both with our weapons drawn. We are focused, although not really expecting an attack but still very much on alert having the memory of that ambush fresh in our minds. I can sense that Mistress is colored all red, I know she is ready, willing and eagerly waiting to kill, rend and maim but not expecting to have to. Her desires are contagious. I hear more than one person on the other side of the door and my finger caresses the turning of my wand that will release death and destruction. But as the door opens I see my brother Cum's smiling face and know all is well. He is followed by three others Slice and that woman from the bar called Dovey as well as my sister Hex. All enter and are cordially greeted by Mistress who feels much more relaxed now, she smiles and I know her happiness.

Standing Mistress goes directly to Dovey to greet her, "Dovey love I'm just so glad you could come. I really wanted an old friend around so I decided to offer the one thing I knew you can never resist, a banquet by

Pepper. But why don't you and Slice go and relax in the bath while I take care of some last minute problems. Cum you assist Dovey and perhaps Crap and Taken can provide a bit more entertainment for the two of you in my sunken tub. Hex I know you want to get back to your researches but could you let Crap know where she should be."

Dovey's beaming smile and lunging grab for Cum establishes her acceptance of Mistress's suggestion and as Taken slides under Slice's arm his grin mirrors hers. I look up at Mistress and stroke the calf of her leg as I know she feels she needs to finish her readings. But just being alone with her even if her mind is leagues away, has become more than enough for me. I curl up round her ankles so pleased and contented that I purr.

XXX

Dovey's entrance into the steamy tub is anything but decorous, rather than empty the tub completely with a jump and a splash; she merely gets naked and rolls in laughing. Even then she causes a near tidal wave to slop over the edges of the pool and sluice down the floor drains. Everyone else jovially and gracefully slides into the bubbling heated aromatic waters but the groups' bulk combined also causes even more water to slop over the edges and drain away. Everyone is able to comfortably stand and expose their naked breasts except Dovey who has to strain on her tip toes in order to keep her head above the water at least until she makes her way to the submerged seating area in the center of the tub. It is there that she perches, pleased as punch and motions for Cum to join her.

Slice just moves over to one side laying his head on the edge and stretching full out to float on his back while Crap and Taken move to join him with big smiles on their faces. Crap leans forward to brush her lips over his as Taken slips between his legs and begins to first blow on his cock then to lick from the base of his shaft up to the tip. His deep voice is softened by the bubbly water noises when he murmurs, "I love Copper's pool almost as much as I adore Copper's girls."

Crap partly sprawled over him answers with a deep kiss holding his head with both of her hands and pressing her chained and ringed nipples into his broad hairy chest while he gently toys on one chain to arouse her lips and clit. Taken teases the very tip of his cock with her lips and her face takes on a delightful aspect, it is almost as if she is savoring a chocolate dipped banana. She uses her hands to help hold his hips afloat but as she becomes engrossed in tasting the banana her nails start involuntarily to dig into his flesh.

Dovey is not even trying to float rather she is straddling Cum's hips with her own thick muscled legs as he is stretched out on the seat with his head safely, if barely above water. Dovey's face is now one of total concentration having given over completely to rutting down on the slave's cock. Cum uses both hands to brace against the seat below and aided by the water buoyancy, he thrusts up into Dovey. The waves caused by the two of them combined with the waves of Slice and the girls whip the water into a frenzy that is matched by the rollicking revelers. Crap now reverses turning to drape herself over Slice's face barely being able find support on the edge of the tub as his lips and tongue soon have her, like the pool, frothing at the hips. Taken fills her mouth and throat with his cock. He shudders and thrusts with more violence as she begins to press her finger into his ass. Suddenly in an instant of unbalance, one of Crap's hands slips from the edge of the tub and all three tumble into the water. They all come up sputtering and laughing but renew their carousals with even greater intensity.

Dovey howling out in near lupine abandon drives herself down on Cum's cock as she reaches out with both hands to drag his face close enough for her to kiss then surrendering, arches back. Louder now the whoops and gasps seem to echo and rebound from the walls just as the waves slosh back and forth in time with the gyrations. Cum's body stiffens as his rod impales Dovey and thrusts her far out of the water, only his lips and nose remain above the surface as he heaves in a last massive surge of his hips. He sinks back under the water until Dovey grabs him hard with both arms around his throat and traps his ear lobe in her teeth. Using both of his hands to support her weight he lifts her and carries her to the pool side where she drapes over the edge exposing her ass to him. Standing behind her, his slick cock enters with ease while his fingers find her engorged clit. As he drives his cock deeper inside and his hand tweaks the little bud, her fingers curl into claws and rake the hard stone floor. She moans and arches her back as he pumps into her driving those flying hips forward into the side of the pool creating waves to expand backwards. Her final extended moan rising in volume until once more she howls out her supreme delight.

On the other side of the pool Slice moves to sit on the edge and leans back as Crap stands behind him. She bends far forward draping herself over top of him so that her inner thighs now frame his face. She continues to bend over, resting her hands on the side of the pool until she is able to capture his cock in her mouth. Taken's fingers once again find Slice's ass and press up hard while her other hand teases Crap's nipple rings, gently tugging on the chains, titillating and engaging all the rings, right down to her clit.

Continuing until spent both Cum and Slice slide once more into the pool. Cum supporting a thoroughly satiated Dovey and Slice showing off by kneeling down and perching both girls on his shoulders before standing up proudly like a conjurer with his familiars on their roosts. This is not the first time that both the brother and sister have given themselves over to gay abandonment with Mistress Copper's slaves and will not be the last as they both know their every wish will be not only fulfilled but their tiniest desire will be happily and enthusiastically met and exceeded. The bubbling waters, warm and fragrant cover them, seething and sloshing over their bodies and through their senses like a drug that buoys their thoroughly satisfied beings. All five having secured once again the shuddering spasms of delight and heady levels of awareness each of them love so well. But both Crap and Taken must now go to the Altar to preserve Slice's sperm and Cum carefully almost reverently dries Dovey's glowing body. Noticeably, as the last of the bathers leave the tub a loud gurgle of rushing water can be heard and the tub rapidly begins to refill.

Chapter Five

Sitting curled around Mistress's feet I hear her gasp and receive the wave of gladness that emanates from her as I feel her mind grasp and hold on to a eureka moment. In that instant she has just come to understand and know what is needed to be done and maybe even how to do it. I look up when she smiles down upon me and says, 'Do you know what I found my sweetling?"

I shake my head, "I only know that you have found an answer but not what the answer is."

"Yes MINE, but this is no easy task and the dangers associated with it are not small but it is better if I tell everyone at once. So I want you to go to Toy and Sugar and ask them both come down for supper. Oh and Doll, make very sure Sugar understands that we can and will make this right." Mistress's genuine concern caresses me like the heat of her breath on my flesh when she holds me close but it also includes such a demanding urgency that my, "Yes Mistress," is but a quick statement as I flee, feet flying from the room.

I run to Mistress's room but enter very quietly and carefully until finding both my sisters awake on the bed with Toy cradling Sugar in her arms. I can easily see the horror and desperation written clearly on Sugars face.

48

They look up when I speak, "Mistress wants you both, sisters". Toy rises to join me but Sugar remains prone on the bed in stunned shock at her predicament. I now have the chance of being the bearer of glad tidings so with a smile to Sugar I say, "She told me to tell you that she has found a way for your voice and scars to be made right, so please come quickly." But coming quickly is not yet to be, for the relief that spread over Sugar's face was beatific and in answer Toy jumps up ramming her fist toward the heavens with a forceful "YES!" Even though Sugar tries to get out of bed quickly enough, she is hampered by Toy's and yes, my hugging. Yet hurry we do, dressing Sugar as fast as we can and also being spurred on by the sensuous wafting of enticing aromas rising up through the door and signaling that supper is about to be served.

The three of us arrive almost at the same time as Taken, Crap, Cum, Mistress's 'Hire Sword' Slice and our guest Dovey who all bound into the room in great spirits. Before us are two wheeled serving carts, the first holding a keg with steins as well as carafes of both red and white wines, surrounded by long stemmed glasses but the contents of the second cart are as wondrous to behold, not only for the mouthwatering display of food but also for the intrigue of who is under the food. For their chained to the table is the thief called Cyril, bedecked, covered, wrapped and ladened as a platter to display all sorts of delectable dishes, treats and condiments.

His hair has been transformed into a Medusa's Crown of snake shaped breads, all rolled and baked to a multi-colored perfection then sprinkled with several contrasting colors of seeds of differing size and shape. This head dress is matched by a pair of bread boots that cover his feet and ankles. These boots use two colors of bread baked together with the darker bread imitating both the laces and the soles of the boots.

His legs are fitted with thin wide pasta noodles, wrapping around his calves and thighs inundated with a combination of bacon strips and swathes of bright green cooked spinach. To add to this colorful wonder, these bizarre leggings are studded with mushrooms and drizzled with a rich red pasta sauce combined with a liberal sprinkling of ground cheeses and peppers.

But his bread medusa's hood and booties and his pasta paneled leggings pale when you looked at his hips, for there standing prominently displayed, almost like a bouquet of flowers in full bloom is a collection of vertically arrayed asparagus shoots, all a uniform eight inches long, bright and green with thin rounds of lemon secured by tooth picks at the very top of each shoot. These lemons slices appear to be yellow open flowers. All of these stalks have been secured like a rampart girding his engorged cock, held securely by tightly stretched rings of large pure white calamari. Rings rising on top of ring all binding both the vegetables and his meat. Scattered liberally, and stacked deeply around his groin are shelled pink shrimps bedded in green sorrel.

But above the waist there is edible meat. Traveling up from his waist to his chest there are racks of ribs stacked all parallel. Each rib aligned with the next, ordered so that the knobby bones overlap along the centerline of his body and the meaty ends draped down over his sides. These ribs with meat barely adhering to the bone have been separately cut and lay with the lower tips of the ribs touching a pile of potatoes, yams, carrots, all garnished with parsley and a smattering of rings of onions.

This collection of vegetables is piled around his chest and arms up to his throat and wrists. While boats of gravy, bowls of flavored oils, melted butter and garlic and rich red seafood sauce are conveniently positioned for dipping on each side of his arms, shoulders and even between his legs. The largest dipping bowl tucked up hard into his groin.

Between each of the ribs are also several crusted chicken wings and drumsticks. These ribs, wings and drums climb up over his belly from his hips almost all the way to his chest to meet the oysters on a half shell and slices of lemon strewn across the top.

The chains may have been visible on his wrists except for the bright red whole lobsters spread out over his lower arms and hands. These feisty flavored crustaceans are supported in part by piles of muscles closely packed around his arms, all open and garnished with pimento, onion and parsley.

While gigantic shrimp tails rise from deep inside of his wide open mouth becoming a shrimp corsage, mangoes, bananas, strawberries and cherries cover his eyes as well around his neck, forehead and chin. His cheeks are dark with the color of chocolate that matches the bowls of liquid chocolate on either side of his head. Chocolate that can be used for dipping

To salute this display of wonderful foods and a well deployed thief, Mistress fills a glass with deep ruby red wine then raising it high declares, "And now, my friends and MINE, supper is served!"

Dovey going over to the trolley first examines the offerings then taking a single stalk of asparagus turns to Pepper saying, "I'm so lucky your Mistress grabbed you before I saw you or they would have to use a wheelbarrow to get me around the bar." Grabbing a giant shrimp she goes over to Pepper and offers it, compelling Pepper to bend far over to taste it. This very action is immediately used by Dovey to grasp Pepper's collar and drag her face that few inches lower and steal a quick kiss.

I do not giggle at the sight of Pepper leaning far over and being kissed by the diminutive Dovey but cannot help to smile when after the kiss, Dovey popped the remains of the shrimp into Pepper's mouth and uses her middle finger to wipe a bit of the garlic butter off of my sister's lips.

I feel Mistress yearning for a strawberry dipped in chocolate. As I take one from his eyes, I'm startled to see Cyril's uncovered eye blink, look at me then wink. Smiling I move to Mistress kneeling before her holding the delicacy aloft for her to take. I feel her in my mind pleased with my actions but then equally pleased with the smooth texture, perfect temperature and subtle flavors of the sweet berry.

Our eyes meet as Mistress bends forward lifting my chin with the tip of her finger and gently presses the glass of wine to my lips saying, "Doll take this glass for your own and bring me back another and a rib or two."

After setting my glass down, I pour fresh wine into a new goblet and return with three large ribs that I have dipped in the sauce. I hand Mistress the wine and two of the ribs and after a nod from her bite into the third. The flavor explodes! It is 'Pepper's Own Brown Sugar, Garlic and Bourbon Sauce'. The Smokey bourbon lashes the succulent meats into drooling submission before it slathered them with the sweetness and richness of garlic's passion.

But in that instant a new thing happened to Mistress and me, we share a flavor both of us echoing the delight to each other. In such close proximity I can sense, almost see the bond of my brand fueling the exchange of the power born by the tastes of sweet, of meat, and of bourbon and garlic. Our eyes meet underscoring the bond but after that instant I feel Mistress draw away and focus on the rest of the feasting group. I too look back and enjoy the happy revelry now in full flight but also catch the pointed and inquiring stare of Hex whose dark eyes bore into me. I slowly nod to her in acknowledgment but not in confirmation of her questing gaze.

Looking around I see that everyone else is already devouring the feast. Dovey seated on a low bench has Cum kneeling before her passionately ripping the meat from a rib bone held securely between her buxom breasts. Over to the side reclining on a cushion is Slice. Both Hex and Crap are sharing the task of anointing his cock with chocolate then licking, teasing and caressing it clean. Feeling somewhat left out, I take a muscle and after digging the meat out with the tip of my tongue use the still joined halves of the shell as a grabber to choose other bits and pieces from Cyril's body and just occasionally nipping his flesh as well. I attack the muscles mostly using the shell grabber to drag the meats and garnishes out of the shells. I then help Pepper feed the lad by dropping a chunk of pasta, bacon and spinach into his mouth, at the same time as winking at him just as he had at me when I took the first strawberry for Mistress. Having gained his attention, I lower my lips to his cock and kiss the tip before tearing a calamari from his straining member with my teeth. Reaching up I take an oyster and let the cold slippery flesh slide down my throat then grab a drumstick and begin to chew as I use the oyster shell to pick up some sweet potato and onion. The combined flavors and relaxed festivities are as truly wonderful as the Mistress's family and friends feast together. But when Pepper hands me a bourbon bottle and I take a short sip everything seems to become even more happy and alive. I thank her with a kiss as we share another drink or three before passing the bottle back to her. But our exchange is cut short by Mistress.

Clapping her hands, "My dear friends, our wonderful platter and Mine, lend me your uncorked ears for a short while."

I can't help but notice the surprise on the thief's face on being addressed at all and know that he as well as the rest of the room has given full attention to Mistress.

"My sweet Sugar was injured while defending my house from a demonic attack. We saved her life but her throat has been so badly violated and scarred that she can barely speak. This must and will be rectified. That demon is now thanks to the aid of Taken and Pepper, in hell and my Spite with her minions will harass and kill the bitch daily. But revenge is just not enough; we need the scars removed and the healing to occur. Hex has discovered an ancient scroll that speaks to the removal of scars set deep into flesh. It even tells us how and where to begin this quest for the healing as well as some vague outline as to the nature that the quest must take, which I might add is just a tad on the buttered up side of unusual."

"Dovey I have asked you here tonight to enlist your aid in this quest as part of it seems to be deep into the catacombs. Your knowledge of that place will aid us immensely should you and I do hope you do, wish to join us."

"Cyril you're a young thief and have quite frankly one of the fastest, most flirtatious and ever glib tongues in you that I have had the fortune and misfortune to hear. If you'll forgive my little prank, I would like to ask you to join us as well. For you and of course Slice and Dovey, I can offer more than ample remuneration for your endeavors as well as my thanks and goodwill."

"Slice I'm counting on you. I once jokingly said that you are, 'No longer on like a john, but rather in like sin!' but now I really do need you to prove that to me. For on our quest we have to go and find the Skeleton King but not to kill him. This is where the writing is somewhat faded on the ancient scroll but I think it suggests that rather than violence, the one needing all scars removed must first steal for him before giving him his head. Now I have several ideas of what that could mean but no idea how that can happen and would be most open to suggestions. Perhaps in finding him we can find that out at that time."

The stunned silence that follows has comical aspects to it, the open mouths, Cyril's skin turning ash white as he continually licks his lips and the dumbfounded expression on Sugar's face. It is Slice that ends all this when he simply stands, grimly smiles and walks over to Cyril, gently grasping the thief's balls and turning back to Mistress saying, "Copper, you and your house hold my loyalties as surely as I hold this thief's lovely balls but even long after I let go this happy handful, you can be sure that he and I will follow where ever you lead or else he can be assured that they will be right back in my not so gentle hands! Right Laddy?"

The appreciation on Dovey's face is evident as she goes to stand opposite her brother, leans over and tears the last calamari off the thieves cock, chewing happily she smiles and says, "You can count on all three of us. Right Laddy?"

I swear I don't even smile when Cyril closes his eyes, gulps then finally nods his head in hopeless resignation. But I take heart and my full glass over to the thief, drinking deeply and carefully before letting him sip wine from my kiss. A short time later speaking as if it is a solemn vow, I murmur, "And this, my friend is how the house of Copper steals the best of bargains."

Mistress then continues, "Pepper the scroll clearly states that no more and no less than ten must accompany the one who is scarred. The ancient scroll is emphatic on this; furthermore someone needs to stay behind. That will be you, not only because you know the magic's to protect the house but also because you could cast to bring your sister Spite to us if needed. This quest will take three or more days and we shall need food for that duration. While you prepare the food, we shall all prepare ourselves so plan for us to leave not tomorrow, but the day after."

As I feel the serious side of Mistress fade into the background, she grins, "Now MINE, you know how I hate to see Pepper's fine foods wasted so get over there and lick that platter clean." As commanded I drop my lips to Cyril's chest and begin to lick the rib sauce away. I suck his nipple between my lips and start to tease with my tongue. Looking into his eyes I can see a look of wonder as seven of us descend on him, our fingers, lips and tongues all reaching, searching and caressing only trying to do our Mistress's bidding but with an enthusiasm all our own.

Pepper merrily comes over with that large bottle of bourbon smiling and winking in apparent innocence before taking a healthy pull and lowering her bourbon filled mouth to his cock; at that instant his eyes open wide, very, very wide, very, very quickly! He might even have spoken, if his lips were not fully covered by Toy's demanding kisses, not that it mattered much as he very rapidly also became the recipient of a zap from Hex.

I am looking at Mistress who is busy talking with both Dovey and Slice, when Hex takes my hand and leads me to the trolley with the wine and beer. She pours a wine glass of a vintage red and laughed as we began to share the deeply dark and delectable wine. Both of our lips are on the rim of the same glass as she murmurs, "We two have not really learned to trust each other yet sister and on this quest we must trust each other completely." Moving her lips to the bottom of my slave collar and licking and sucking. "I'm sure we can find a way to learn more of each other."

The wine, the bourbon, the good food only turns our closeness into desire as I reach to tug her to me by her chains. She slips off her robe and takes me in her arms pressing our ringed hard nipples together. My breath comes sharply now as I feel myself being carried away on a rushing wave of passion. Somehow I become turned around and I find myself swaying almost staggering in her embrace. Suddenly, without warning my earlobe screams in pain! Hex has bitten down hard and to my horror we both watch as Mistress grabs her own ear.

My hairless sister Hex chuckles before releasing me whispering, "I now know your secret sister but it is safe with me. Now come, we two need to talk." She grabs a carafe of wine and another glass in one hand before asking me by the shoulder with the other. Looking back as Mistress nods to us, I smile at Hex and leave the room to go down to her chamber.

We go down not one but two levels to Hex's large room. She invites me in with a flourish and a shove causing me to stagger a bit. My sister passes me a silver flask. Taking a sip I find an entirely different kind of whiskey, one that holds a smoky tinge of heaven or perhaps a heady sort of hell.

"This slave saw you and Mistress, sister; this slave saw what you both share. Your branding has changed you; it has made you feel like part of Mistress. This slave has read of this several times so can understand a little. But your sister needs to know more, can you tell me how this works between you?"

I hesitate as I look around the room seeing the many ornate book cases, the numerous jars of things that look disquieting, a small laboratory table, the carpets, skulls and candles placed in the center of the floor and a slave pen for her to rest in. Taking a long sip and savoring the flavor I turn and state flatly, "Mistress instructed me not to tell any others of her house, sister. Do not ask this sister to disobey, please don't. I beg you."

"That is now understood sister; Mistress works hard to make sure we are all loved. But to keep the secret safe Mistress will let me help you, she knows of all of her slaves' loyalties." Looking at me openly, smiling tenderly Hex continues, "You have never been to this room have you sister, long ago an earlier resident of this house used this room for his laboratory and library. It has been commanded that this slave continue his work. This slave has for years sought to understand the mysteries of this land. But now in some way parts of these mysteries are unfolding because of you sister."

"The shot you made killing one of those damn birds has given this searcher the greatest clue any have had for many generations." Going over to the small table she picks up a small gold and white object and returns with it. "This, what ever it is was inside the bird you killed. That kill has never, in all the research done by so many of us before, been successful. This artifact appears to be both electrically designed and magically powered but it must also store it's own information for there seems to be no other way of communicating the data, furthermore there is just no way of knowing its purpose or even whose directions it follows. All this is a mystery. This mystery is starting to unfold because you. You managed that shot and now somehow you have become an empath. Mistress knows and approves of the search this slave has pursued sister so take heart, in time it all shall be explained. But there is another thing that you should know." Moving to the oldest looking book case she strokes the lower edge causing a grating sound to rise up through the stone floor. The stone slab in the center of the summoning carpets drops down and slides away leading to a hidden stair case.

"When Mistress bought this house she found this door open as if the last resident had left in a hurry or tried to as there were several sets of bones found in the tunnel. The tunnel entrance was as far as Mistress wished me to explore and somehow she seems to have forgotten all about the rest of it. But I recently found a map which tells us that the tunnel leads many miles underground to a forest where ancient limestone pillars are standing in a circle. This is to be the last escape from this house sister, to be used only when all else fails."

I am beginning to feel giddy now, my sister is swaying back and forth and my head is getting hot but my stomach is rolling up and down. I lean on my sister saying, "This one is not feeling well sister, her stomach is trying to fight its way out." Hex's urgency is apparent as we leave the room going up the first set of stairs to a lavatory where my belly tries to explode through my mouth, mostly succeeding.

My sister holds by shoulders and hair back as I wretch out my innards into the porcelain throne I am kneel in front of. Hex washes my sweating face then helps me back up the stairs. They were perfectly good stairs before but now they seem to be crooked and lumpy. I cannot stand or walk on them right, I actually tried to ask Hex who had cursed the stairs but it came out pretty muddled so I though it better just to be helped to my pen. I lay down for a minute to allow my belly to settle down but my eyes do not want to open again.

Chapter Six

The dimly lit pall that extends over the gravel strewn caves of Niffelem offers a bit of cover that only the most careful can use, for all others the constantly shifting surface betrays every step with the harsh rattling grind of gravel on stone. That does not hinder the party of five demons that walk with purpose, tridents out and glowing with their protective spells. They have one leader and one purpose, to attack and destroy the bodily form of Macey.

I lead them and walk proudly striving for my most regal and demonic manner possible, that I wear the collar identifying me as 'Copper's Spite' is not at issue; rather that I have noble standing and appear to be in command is the most important. I glare at the caverns of this plane with purpose. My nobility is like a flag I hold aloft. It is that which lets those who walk with me know of my deep seated rage, hatred and solemn purpose. A hatred that must be perceived as going far beyond the normal simple feud between Succi and Inq; my every movement must be seen as stored resentment and every minor impediment even so small as a bit of gravel must serve as only to fuel the fires of my bitterness. Even the smallest rock is ground to dust under my stomping hooves. We advance as a cohort finding in our path collections of undead some who stupidly try to take a stand against us; they die and their screams echo in our ears, others just flee. Our group comes to a doorway cut into a solid rock face. The locks take mere seconds to breach before the five of us are through the door in a rush.

Macey our prey has no chance to even react as four magically strengthened demons grab her hooves and arms stretching her painfully spread eagled on the floor. She tries to struggle; laughing in her face, I deliberately and personally demonstrate the hopeless of her position by tearing her clothes from her. Aside from stripping her I only grin as she is held there naked for all to see. She tries to threaten but is greeted by silence. She tries to bargain but is ignored. Standing over her I see her sharply inhale when finally she sees the writing on the collar at my throat. Then and only then do I gently press my trident to her throat. Groaning in recognition she looks up saying, "You know I had no choice in this, no more than you would have had."

Even more angry now, if it is possible she is trying to compare herself to me; I snarl with my fangs scant inches from her face, "My sister Sugar is almost as dear to me as Mistress! When I was mortal before your brother cut my heart out, she and I loved, learned, fought together and saved each other's lives many times. In that long ago, it was just her and I, and together we danced and whored our way through most of the bars in London, picking pockets and rolling drunks as we went. Until one day a few men decided we had to work for them. In a bar five of them bound and stripped us then tried to leash us, until Mistress Copper alone stood and took out her whip. She worked and wielded it until they all ran. A day later Sugar and I went to Mistress Copper and we both knelt before Mistress to offer our throats together. You almost killed her but you failed. I will not let you return to London to try again." Smiling I drive my trident deep into the her belly, then again into her chest skewering her through both breasts, before I use the last and killing thrust this time into her throat. Black blood spurts up and out with each attack but its flow decreases quickly, leaving me only scant seconds to reach forth with a vial and scoop out some of the hearts blood from her trident ruined chest.

I turn to the other four and dismiss them, "Now with this blood, I alone can track her! You have done your duty well and later I shall reward each of you, but for now return to your romps while I hunt alone. I shall be the Harridan that harries her through all the hells, tracking, attacking and killing her again and again."

The five of us leave the Spartan apartment and my companions cast their spells allowing them to transport home. I briefly seat myself on the hard gravel and concentrate on the vial of heart's blood, when I eventually look up I can feel myself smiling darkly. I stand then cast the spell that transports me to Hades the plane where Macey had been thrown by my first murder of her today.

I know from personal experience the problems she faces now. I know that she is in trouble and she is fully aware of it. The Inquisitor will be naked, weaponless and have no way of contacting friends. Finding her will not be a problem now that I have her heart's blood, I have several other ways of tracking, but taking some heart's blood provides me the easiest of all. And find her I do, it takes me all of a half a dozen minutes to catch up with her just outside the 'First Satanic Bank of Trust Lust and Betrayal'. That would have been a place of some refuge for her but I get there first and wait until at the last second before she enters I step forth and bar her way.

"Going to pick up your toaster luvey? Not on my watch you don't! You are about to learn just how nasty I can be." I can see the fear in her eyes now, I know how much depends on keeping that look there and I will not let that go. "Let me tell you your future. According to Mistress, I don't have to kill you again until tomorrow. You see, she would only have me prevent you from being summoned by your brother or his minion; but that was Sugar you attacked. You have made this very personal so I'm going to keep on killing you until by sheer random chance we arrive back on my home plane. After that you will to be spending some time in my dungeon paying for your sins against my sister. Do you understand me now bitch?"

Macey backing away, holds up her hands in front of her face palms outward as if to shield herself from an attacker. "I have no weapons; I can't fight you like this. If you want to make this worth your while give me armor and a weapon so we can settle this with honor."

"Honor! You? A holy hypocrite babbles on about armor and weapons? What right do you have to ask for anything? You have made yourself my enemy. You will learn what a very bad thing that is to do because I do not fight for honor, only to win. I'm not like the caring mortal my Mistress is, she hates suffering even in enemies. I don't have that little limitation and actually I'm going to love to watch you suffer. It may have been your brother who carved my heart out but it was you who used your talons on my sister." My words begin to drip with anger and hatred. "You talk of honor!" I give a coughing laugh. "That's just not happening. I'm going to truly enjoy hearing every scream you utter as I chase you from plane to plane." She turns to bolt but her action is not quick enough. In a single motion I grab her hair, pulling back and down allowing her only to look up while the other hand slams the butt end of my trident deep into the hard packed ground. Having one hand free I grab her wrist pulling it violently behind her back before I move her head far enough forward allowing her to gaze in horror at the trident's position. Holding Macey's hair hard I keep her head in a single spot lifting her captured wrist and breaking her arm and then slam her forward to impale her belly on the three tines of the trident. Releasing her wrist to allow her arm to hang at a cruel crooked angle I laugh as the life seeps away from her and watch her eyes as she dies once more. I rapidly seat myself and concentrate before smiling and returning to stand and cast again, this time transporting myself to Armageddon.

I successfully land just steps behind her and take a war whip in hand. She has not even seen me as the whip's lash encircles her throat. She freezes as she hears my voice.

"Got you now and I'll get you again! You can't even manage to run from me." I allow her enough time to sob once before I yank on the whip severing the arteries and veins in her throat. Again I seat myself and rapidly find her before flying between the planes to catch her again. I wonder how many times I will be able to do this today, relishing the thoughts of not only the pain, suffering and hurt I am inflicting on her but the mental anguish and frustrations I am working even harder to deliver.

This time she sees me and runs, working hard to try and stay far enough in front of me to avoid my whip. She may be naked and not carrying the weight of armor as I am but the constant attacks have weakened her. I catch her with some ease and attack this time not looking for a swift kill but rather chasing and lashing her causing great pain and deep wounds. Many ragged strips of skin hang from her back, legs and arms, with the special attention that I give to her ass; it is now a bloody pulp and causes her to writhe on the ground. Finally, I go over to her and just stomp down hard on her forehead crushing her skull with a vengeance.

I chase her down again and again, each time when I see her I notice that she is becoming more drawn and exhausted. Her face is now showing panic and defeat she is so weak that she is shaking. I notice that she is approaching a point beyond panic. She is now feeling the mind numbing terror that only repeated defeat and destruction can bring. Macey has finally realized that there is no respite for her anywhere. She turns and staggers towards me falling to her knees lowering her head to the inevitable saying, "Go ahead, I cannot stop you. If it is your wish I will even surrender to you.

I only ask for quick deaths and the strength not to cower before your whips and blades."

Smiling at her while putting away my whip I take out a smaller blade, grab her hair and take the time to slowly and painfully saw through the tough flesh of her throat. After her dead body again slumps to the ground I once more sit, take out the vial and concentrate. Fifteen minutes later on the Norse of plane of Hel I again find Macey; she can barely stand now her legs and arms shaking violently from exhaustion as I force her to kneel before me. This time Macey grits her teeth, quietly sobs once before she lowers her head saying, "I give you my surrender, my promise to never attack your sister Sugar again. I offer these freely and without reservation."

I had not expected this. I have to take a step back in surprise. I feel my hackles rising; this is a game changing move on her part, one I have to view with great suspicion.

"You are willing to not only surrender but give your word never to attack again?" I wanted this, perhaps too much to trust her words. But for her to surrender to me a noble and have that surrender rejected would reduce my stature in all of hell. Seeing no other choice I take command by quickly walking behind her and tightly shackling her elbows together. "You're coming with me now; I'm taking you to my dungeon. I will accept your surrender but do not expect that your bed will be a soft one, for what you made today you will lie naked in until I say otherwise."

I am fully aware of the Inquisitors fear and disgust for nudity and casual sex of any kind. I know her nakedness may have had some bearing on her surrender. In order to confuse her further, I take my cloak and wrap it over her shoulders, for no other reason than it is the last thing she expects and the first thing she would want. Taking a hold on the chains binding her I cast and return to my own plane.

Chapter Seven

My first inkling that I am awake is not so much a coherent thought as a moan, dredged up from a pain filled kind of despair. "Owww", my head feels like it is being squeezed in a red hot vise, my throat is parched and tastes like the bottom of a bird cage but the second sensation I feel is my nipple being sucked and my clit feels like someone is teasing it. My head is throbbing but my body is on fire with the sensations and feelings of being well and truly fucked. Not really awake I open my eyes a crack to see who is with me but my poor befuddled brain cannot understand the fact that I am all alone in my pen. Looking around bleary eyed I can see and hear no other soul about me.

Somehow through the bombardment of conflicting sensations I crawl from my pen and grab the pitcher of water. Taking the pitcher in both hands, pouring part of it down my throat and the rest over my head helps ease the parching in my throat but does nothing for my confused mind. Standing there I still feel as if I am coming ever closer to an orgasm. I really don't know what is happening here. Did one of my sisters 'Zap' me then sneak away? Surely they were not that nasty? If only I can try to find the most comfortable position to overcome this horrible hangover I may survive and understand. I can barely even think with the sensations racing through my body and the pounding of hammers in my head. If one of my sisters has zapped me when I am this hungover she is going to be switched from my 'nice list' directly to my 'naughty list'.

I feel it, the calm assurance that all is right, the lust for possession of another and the sheer strength and pride that can come from only one person, Mistress! I am feeling what she is feeling. Understanding now, I am not just miserably hungover but my body is being aroused by the actions of a sister giving pleasure to Mistress. Crawling from my pen I stagger unsteadily out of the room determined not to let Mistress feel my discomfort and head straight for the bath in order to slide gratefully into the reviving steamy waters. Floating there while the gentle aromas sooth my pains I relax and close my eyes. My body seems at war, the arousal and the sensations are in conflict with my roiling stomach and aching head. Partly submerged all I can hear is the gentle bubbling of waters around me where I feel some easement of my pain accompanied by the sinful secondhand delights of being made love to. I recognize and indulge myself in the sensation of feeling and being aroused by a stroking that does not even touch my body. These sensations allow me to savor the memories of the manner and nature of Crap's love making. I had never really realized I could identify a sister by how she made love but laying there in the water I revel in the thoughts that I live with such wonderfully sisters, all uniquely different. My pain has just started to fade and morph into the lust created by Mistress when I become aware that others are entering the pool. Not really caring who, I open a bleary eye and see Taken hand in hand with Slice alongside Pepper and Cyril as they all slide into the pool; moreover both Dovey and Cum are right behind them.

My single painful eye notes that Dovey is carrying a jug of something, she takes one good look at the lot of us and with an agonizingly loud cackle announces, "Well, me oh my, I can't remember the last time I saw so many sorry hangovers in one tub." Then with loud and ill-concealed glee she almost shouts, "But fear not, for Dovey is here to save the day." On that booming proclamation she nods to Cum who pours out tumbler sized glasses of foul looking sludge for everyone. "This is my special recipe and you have got to promise to instruct everyone you ever see with a hangover that they have to come to HFC and beg me for this elixir, their last best hope for salvation. Now pay attention! For this to work fastest and best, you never, ever look at it. The sight of it has alone has caused cookies to hurl in the past. Also do not even dream of smelling it, for to taste this is a really! And I do mean really bad thing. So close your eyes hold your nose then get it all down at once." With that she raises her own glass high, holds her nose and pours the tumbler into her open mouth as fast as she can swallow. I can feel Craps tongue inside Mistress and I'm so close to cumming that I can't wait but I drain the drink on the spot so aroused I hardly notice the disgusting taste. Then in a single instant before I get a secondhand orgasm I duck my head under the water and squeeze myself hard trying to contain my moans. At least I have not let the others know what is happening because hungover or not, I would have no clue as to how I would explain this to my sisters. Holding my breath as long as I can I finally pop my head above the water and realize that not only is Mistress nicely satisfied but that wonder of wonders my hangover is gone as well.

Thanking Dovey profusely I start to leave but am detained by Pepper when she reaches up to take my hand. She pulls me close enough to whisper in my ear, "Sister stay with us a while, I have to go start cooking for Sugar's Quest but I'm very sure our thief friend would like to get to know you better." Winking she reaches down to squeeze the cheek of my ass before climbing out of the tub and blowing a kiss to all as she makes her way to the towel rack.

Smiling first at Pepper then at Cyril, secretly knowing that Mistress is still very preoccupied with Crap I go over to ruffle his hair but before I get there Slice reaches out to take my hand, guiding me to his side.

I giggle as he pulls me close and begins to kiss my throat saying, "I have not had enough of your company girl but we can make up for that this morning."

I am intrigued, wondering if Mistress will also experience what I feel as I had just shared with her such a short time ago. I really don't want to intrude upon her but it is a puzzle that I am drawn to. So leaning forward I nuzzle and kiss my way down to his naval with my chin in the water. I kiss, nibble and lick at his belly as my hands seek out and find his shaft. He hardens rapidly but totally surprises me when one of his hands slides between my thighs and I am lifted out of the water to sit on his shoulders. My hips are pulled into his waiting face where his tongue stabs me to the core and I quickly grab at his head to keep myself from falling back into the pool. This is really helpful as he slowly bends forward while using both of his hands to continue to make my hips become one with his face. My upper body slowly arches back towards the water until I feel the top of my head becomes partly submerged. Without warning my head is supported and I open my eyes to find it resting easily on Taken's breasts with her lips lowering to meet mine. Slice's hands now eagerly spread my hips wider as I am impaled by his thrusting tongue, at the same time Taken's tongue twines with mine sliding over and around my mouth like a questing snake searching for supper. The bubbles in the tub seemed to roar in my ears as Slice begins to use his lips and tongue to play with my three rings, the same three rings Mistress had used to adorn my lips and clit. It is not that the chains and rings were no longer painful, for they still can make me yelp but rather they bring such a brilliant burst of bright awareness that not having them seems alien to me now. Slice may have been big, strong and a close friend of Mistress who has shown his loyalty before but his tongue, oh yes! Now that is perfection. The kiss from Taken, the teasing tongue of Slice and now the silver threads reaching to me from Mistress's own arousal intertwine like ropes through my body and mind driving me rapidly into a state of higher and higher sensation. Moaning into the kiss as my tongue twists with Taken's, my body shudders with pleasure so violently even my thighs are trembling as Slice finally lowers me onto his cock, thrusting hard and entering me fully. I explode, my head rolls back free from Taken's kiss as I thrust my hips hard into Slice's groin.

On the other side of the tub Dovey and Cum are beginning to make some major waves of their own and Cyril for lack of anything better to do moves over and begins to stroke her ample breasts.

There is a place in all of us, a deep secret place, one that connects our body and our mind, it is there where our hopes, our fears and our desires abide that place is where I can hear Mistress's screams echoing with my own as we both seem to shine as brightly in my mind as two stars going nova at the same instant. Together we illuminate that part in all of us that is small and deep, bringing light and lust into being. In that instant I had connected with Mistress again. I see through her eyes my sister Crap's inner thighs still all a quiver; as she sees Cyril being held and used by Dovey at the edge of the pool. I detect just a hint of possessiveness. Could it be? Yes it must, Mistress has her sights set on Cyril's throat. As the vision fades I know that I must act for Mistress.

I collapse from Slice just after he thrusts into my submerged hips one last time, his sperm filling me. Panting I kiss Taken and then whisper, "I must go sister." As I move from her she goes to Slice while I move toward Dovey. I speak softly and slowly to Dovey and Cyril, "Mistress must be up by now and I'm sure she would like to have those not of her house to join her."

Grinning at Cyril then back at me, Dovey just winks, "Take him to Copper love I'm going to go find your brother again and let him know there is a new day dawning, just in case anything else besides the sun is still rising."

I smile and bow my head in thanks to Dovey. Standing directly in front of Cyril I casually roll my shoulders back giving a small grin as his eyes fasten on my erect nipples and the rings and chains that hold them. Gently taking his hand leading him to the side before climbing out of the tub, I hasten to grab some towels and hold one open for Cyril as he stands looking somewhat pleased to be escaping Dovey's more amorous and aggressive attentions. Carefully and dutifully I dry his body and while I may have spent a suitably excessive amount of time drying those parts of him, that make him, a him, I can hardly take my eyes off the intricate tattoo on his chest and arms. I help him to dress but as I had not thought to bring my own clothing I have no reluctance to proudly display my brand, rings and chains and accompany him naked. Not taking his hand this time, I merely motion for him to follow and as I lead him teasing him with my own bouncing bottom to Mistress's room.

We are greeted by not only Mistress and Crap but also by Hex and Sugar. The smile Mistress uses to welcome me makes it very clear that she approves of my bringing of Cyril to her. In response to her smile and to acknowledge her as my owner and Mistress I kneel before her in the manner first taught to me. With the soles of my feet together and my knees far apart I thrust my hips forward and expose my collar for her leash as I have pledged to her, gratefully placing myself completely and totally at her disposal. Cyril whose appreciation of what he sees elevates as fast as my hips fly forward, smiles and licks his lips.

Raising her hand she calls to Cyril, "Now then my young friend I believe that you and I need to chat. So sit yourself down at the edge of my bed because I want you to understand me."

I can see her endearing smile and feel a pang of jealousy as she invitingly reaches out to him bringing him to sit very close to her. Her hands trace the tattoos through his open fronted shirt and I notice his pants begin to tighten below his waist. Then speaking in the low throaty voice I love so dearly, Mistress continues as she gently strokes him, "First I really have to say what an outstanding platter you made. I can't remember when I have seen so many enjoying so much fun while eating supper. You helped do that and I'd like to thank you for making last evening such a success."

Reaching over slowly she gently strokes his face with the back of her first two fingers then deliberately smiles, her lips scant inches from his before once more leaning back. "You don't have to thank me for including you on Sugar's quest. We both know that you are going to gain far more than you could by trying to steal kisses in the underground. I admit that Slice and Dovey's enthusiasm for you joining us may have been a tiny bit over the moon but we really do need you there and I assure you that you will be rewarded well." Then pondering reflectively Mistress murmurs, "I'm sure you will really enjoy getting to know my House better as well and being on a quest with us shall certainly help you do exactly that."

He responds quickly to Mistress's gentle words with, "I would have come but Slice just sort of made it official."

Mistress continues in a sterner tone, "You must realize that normally I would not even give you the time of day but you have shown at least a glimmering of promise, which is why you are alive and did not suffer my whip."

Cyril instantly glances over at the weapon rack on the wall and gives a bit of a gulp at the mention of the large whip but his eyes quickly return to hers.

"Now you have a chance to not only profit but also to prove yourself to me; do not toss this opportunity away for it will not come again." Almost as an afterthought Mistress grins at me instructing, "Doll my sweetling take our slippery fingered friend down to the kitchen I'm sure that Pepper could use both your help in preparing the fare for the journey. That will also probably get you both fed faster than any other way."

Taking Cyril to the kitchen is easier said than done, not that he is not willing enough but rather because all of a sudden he is full of questions. Little things mostly like, "What does she mean by 'suffer my whip'?" and, "What does she really mean by 'getting to know my House better'?" He would have kept on prattling but I stopped abruptly and putting on my best 'I'm just a poor dumb slave girl look' say, "This slave knows not her Mistress's wishes, only what she is told so come let us help Pepper." Finally after having to kiss him to keep him from further talking we make it to the kitchen.

Entering we see Pepper cleaver in one hand wearing only a heavy leather apron that drops from her breasts to her knees and a very unhappy look. Glancing at Cyril I see that he seems to be totally enchanted by her apron which has left her back bare from her hairline to her heels. I quietly ask, "Sister, Mistress has suggested that Master Cyril and this slave assist you today. How may we best help?"

With a slight look of relief but still not happy Pepper turns first to Cyril saying, "There is charcoal in that black keg; those ten small bags beside it need to be half full of the charcoal so everyone will have their own water purifier." Then handing me a sharp knife, "Sister the quest will need 60 packs of large chopped carrots and celery, for I'll not see the family go with vegetables for three days. Cut enough for one meal, then wrap each in this damp cloth but do it sixty times so that each portion will be separate as well as easy to get at and use. Also Cyril after you are done filling those water purifiers, be very sure to rinse each of them until the water runs clear."

Pepper did not seem to be her normal happy self, seeing the pout on her lips I wince at the rapid chops of her cleaver.

Putting down my knife I go over and place a hand on her shoulder hoping to offer a bit of comfort to my sister and say, "Mistress needs someone to stay home, it probably should be me but I can't cast the spells to summon Spite." I can see her tears starting but see also her bitten lip followed by clenched teeth.

"Mistress has chosen well she always does but this slave fears this quest, it's going to a place where few return from. To stay and be left alone, waiting is so hard, if the house of Copper ends that is the true horror for this slave for she would be left all alone. To be left alone without a Mistress or family, no family to feed, its better she dies with the family than alone and unloved. But this slave will try to do her best making sure everyone has the food they need and working hard not too spend her time in worry but the last is so hard. Promise me sister that whatever happens, keep Mistress safe!"

Cyril watches us while I bring my cheek next to her shoulder saying, "Sister my life belongs to Mistress, I can do nothing else, for that is in this mind both waking and sleep. Fear not, sister for anything that needs doing will be done." With that I return to my chopping and wrapping this time my blade falls faster and harder slashing the food with purpose and energy.

It took the three of us most of the day, for after chopping came grinding seeds and grains together then mixing with raisins, oils and spices, these had to be baked, portioned out and packed. Cyril had helped also by not only cutting strips of meats and seasoning them under Peppers instruction but also by laying them out and watching them carefully before turning them to dry in the largest of the ovens. All this had to be packaged up individually so every person carried their own. All of us had put in a good days work yet when Hex arrives she bears an even greater burden to be dealt with, the dreaded lists, lists of what each person had to have with them and a pen to check off each and every item.

Off I went with Cyril in tow selecting all the things on the list for not only myself but Cyril as well. His gratitude is sweet when he thanks me but I know what he really wants is a kiss which I placed on his lips as the last item is packed and checked off the list.

I had thought that having a whole day before the quest was maybe a bit much but I notice that the oil in the lamps is getting low as we are just finishing. Looking around the common room everyone has their packs by the walls and a list full of checks at the top finally it seems we have reached a state of readiness. Mistress examines every pack and each list in detail. I can feel her need to have everything perfect before we leave, with every list she checks I know she is becoming more confident and in greater control.

There is suddenly the sound of a creaky door opening that seems to be coming from a leather pouch on Mistress's belt. I look at the offending noise maker unsure as whether to be alarmed or not. But Mistress merely takes out a small device and flips it open, before a broad grin spreads over her face.

"This is great news MINE, Spite has succeeded beyond my imaginings. She just texted my Hell-Phone to say that she has captured the demoness Macey and has her under complete control. This at least means no demonic attacks on our quest from that quarter."

I am engulfed by a literal wave of confidence from Mistress. She now believes the quest will be without the same level of danger. Finally after a meticulous inspection and the good news from Spite she turns to us all saying, "We are ready and tomorrow we leave before dawn so all of you get some sleep for tomorrow will be a very long day."

Getting down on my knees in front of Mistress I press my face to her feet softly saying, "Yes Mistress." Tiredly I rise and leave more exhausted that I had realized almost crawling to my pen and there gratefully drop off to sleep.

Feeling as though I had only just closed my eyes, I'm up and joining the other ten assembled in the common room before dawn. Everyone is fully armed and armored but even a journey must start with sustenance. Pepper has been busy for many hours as the breakfast served is piping hot and delectable as only she can make it. Fresh rolls that have been stuffed with a delightful scrambling of eggs, cheese, chives, bacon and garlic is accompanied by bowls brimming with fruit sprinkled with the finest powdered sugar. There are hot croissants heavily loaded with finely sliced smoked salmon topped by capers and standing beside all is a towering urn of freshly brewed coffee.

Pepper herself seems to be frenetically dashing between everyone making sure that we have enough of everything. But it is not difficult to see by her drawn face that it has been stained with many tears this past night. Finally after our last cups of coffee she tightly hugs each of us reluctant to let us go. She whispers in my ear to remember to keep my promise when she embraces me and I squeeze her very hard in response. At last she kneels before Mistress and in a voice almost chocked with tears wishes her a safe journey.

Mistress reaches down, pulling her to her feet and holds her upright looking directly into her eyes, "MINE you know by now to trust me in all things. I know this is difficult but trust me you must! Now clean this up and prepare the protections of my house for that is what I trust you will do."

Pepper chokes back a sob, grabs a tray and rushes from the room as we heft our packs onto our backs; Mistress addresses us bringing our attention to Dovey, "My good friend and old companion has with her brother and Cyril, decided to join our endeavor. I am thankful to have such good friends with us but there is one thing that any of you who have never fought alongside Dovey must know. Never ever get too close to Dovey in battle. Firstly her wand has a wicked side spray, it does not have the normal range of a wand but its damage covers a greater area but secondly." Here Mistress stops and seemingly puzzled as if trying to find the right words then gives up and grabbing a chair says, "Showing is easier that telling. Would you demonstrate Dovey?"

The events that occur next surprise and startle us as Mistress picks up a chair and throws it at Dovey. Dovey does not duck or dodge the oncoming chair but rather slaps the tongue that juts out from her lip shaped belt buckle, flexes here knees and hops into the air spinning as she bounces up. To our surprise her Tutu like skirt made of tapered pink painted metal strips snaps up and stays horizontal to her body, changing her pirouette like spin into a quickly revolving saw of metal strips that cut the chair into splinters before it reaches her.

Mistress winks at us all then with a grin says, "Needless to say, Dovey's skirt can cut through legs just as easily and has many times in the past. So if there is smelly stuff flying from the fan you must remember one thing, STEP AWAY FROM THE FAT ONE!"

After that demonstration I can't help but take a look closer at the laughing Dovey and her armor. She does not wear the same war sandals as Mistress but rather very flat shoes with a partly pointed toe. She uses the same interlocking mail strands as I do but her torso is completely covered with overlapping plates of metal and ceramic, edged by sparking diamond dust these are joined to the metal belt of her tutu like skirt. This wide belt has a buckle that looks like pursed lips slightly open, with the tip of a tongue sticking through almost as if they are about to kiss someone. This is topped by a short cape that falls only to the small of her back. But the most shocking of all is the color of both the metal and the fabric. To say shocking is an understatement for the whole outfit is a vividly bright pink. My own armor which I still believe is the most beautiful ever made is much more revealing but no one can deny that if the two of us stand together all eyes would go to Dovey first.

With a nod Mistress is at last satisfied and leads us through the door allowing us to descend to Hex's room. Hex welcomes us to her private room often referred to as 'Hex's Hole' and glances around saying, "This passage has been here for as long as London. I have never explored it as the writings I have found speak only of dangers and the destination. It will take us out of London to deep underneath an ancient monument. The place called by the ancients 'Stonehenge'. It's where the scroll on the parchment tells us to look for the first clue." Turning from us to the stone trap door on the floor Hex casts a spell unsealing it before going over to the ancient book case and once again she strokes the lower edge. The stone drops away and slides to one side, exactly as it had done in a hazy memory from the night before. As a party we proceed down the deeply cut stone steps.

Mistress has assigned the lead to me with Hex and Slice behind. I can feel her confidence in me as I get to the bottom of a long stairway; she has told me to let my mind see as I had with the nightingale, we will then stand the best chance of traveling unmolested. I am not that confident but Mistress knows far more than I.

I hold my wand in both hands ready to fire instantly. Hex and Slice directly behind me shine reflective lanterns to light the way ahead. I try hard to listen, I need to try to recreate the way my mind worked after the attack so I can sense what lays ahead but distractingly I find myself party to the many worries Mistress holds inside her. I give a shudder at the enormity of the venture as she perceives it, something of great risk that can turn deadly at any second but a venture that unless taken will leave us all less than we have been. I fight back tears for Mistress and struggle to focus on anything that might be ahead of us. My eyes are so tear filled I can hardly see what is directly in front of me. The lamps behind me send out beams of bright light that reflects back from every glistening drop of moisture on the walls and many reflective bits of stone. Seeing with my eyes is becoming very difficult!

Wait! A breath of cool damp air slides between the links of the mail covering my thighs raising a hundred tiny hairs to attention. The draft continues up my torso finally reaching my chin. I freeze mid step and look down, there is only a hard floor in front of me. Puzzled I move the leg that has not yet touched the ground back and the draft is gone. I silently motion every one behind me to move back as I get down on my knees and feel the floor in front of me. Patting the hard rough dusty surface past the spot where my last footprint can be seen in the dust, I see the dust stirred by my actions on the floor suddenly puff away in a draft. I pat only twice more and my hand passes unhindered into the floor.

Chapter Eight

Deep in hell and even deeper in Spite's dungeon, Macey hangs chained. She is hung by both her arms widely spread. She had been able to stand but when the chains Spite had placed on her ankles were tightened they had pulled her legs so far apart that her hooves were left dangling above the floor. She does not know for sure how long she has been there but the pain in her hands, arms and shoulders has turned to numbness. It is black, not the black of night or even the black of when you close your eyes but rather a darkness so complete, even the memory of light has been banished. That ends suddenly when the door opens and Spite and her slave walk in holding bright lamps high in the air. Macey closes her eyes to not only the illumination invasion as her eyes feel physically assaulted by that much brightness but also to the knowledge of being seen in so much light as she hangs in Spite's Dungeon totally naked and totally exposed. As the footsteps move closer there can be heard only whimpers of, "Please mercy, my arms are being torn out of their sockets."

Looking back at my slave Boyo I snicker for effect, before turning to Macey and slapping her face, "Open your eyes, now!" I will not give her that much ease and hold my lamp higher so that when she does reluctantly open her eyes the light is directly in her face. Turning to examine her shackles I see that she has not lied, her hands do have the slightest tinge of blue but this blue is an almost dead blue grey not the cold sky blue she would display in London and her shoulders do seem to be pulling away from her arms.

I have to let her know of my resolve; she has to understand that hope is not an option for her. "Yes I see you are right, soon your arms will be quite useless for anything. Not exactly a bad idea as you could never really attack anyone after that. I should imagine five or six hours more and you'll be crippled for life." I look into her eyes and growl, "A very small repayment for taking my sister's voice. But we don't want you to lose everything right away so I'm going to turn you the other way round and see how long it takes for your hips and legs to give way."

I go to one side and motion to Boyo to take the other and slowly we let the demoness down to the floor. She can't really struggle to stop us as her arms are all but useless now but it is a matter of scant seconds work to switch the chains from her wrists to her ankles and raise her once again. Her face becomes flushed as she moans. The pain of blood rushing back into her arms will be excruciating so further punishment is not required. However, a different kind of stimulation definitely is.

Casting a 'Zap' spell on her now will start her into a whole new appreciation of pain both physical and mental when her multiple orgasms tear through her. Using the word of power very softly and gesturing where she cannot see me I cast, I go to her and run my switch over her labia and clit, stroking gently. Giving a half laugh I croon, "You have spent your whole life as an Inquisitor, to me that means a lifetime of denial, but it may be that I am wrong. Perhaps your way has merit or perhaps it is as we say that really Inq's are merely 'holy hypocrites'. So today we are going to see what you're really made of, are you a frigid iceberg or is there a part of you that really does want to be alive." Walking around in front of her, her face inverted below me but looking upwards displaying the horror of such carnal activities she feels and tells me I have found the perfect nerve. I can cause her body all the pain I want but now the pain I must evoke has to come from deep inside her mind. Teasing her pubic hairs with the very tip of my talon I whisper softly to her, "You are in the power of a true Succi now and I am lust incarnate perhaps if your howls of passion exceed your howls for mercy I'll allow you to keep your arms a while longer." The pain is now evident in her eyes and on her face from the blood rushing into her arms and hands. Motioning Boyo to me I instruct, "Boyo luv I want you to raise her head and shoulders up a little bit, I don't want all of her blood rushing to her head." I smirk when she sees his face and recognition of him dawns on her.

"I see you recognize my Boyo, he was one of your brother's pupils. He must have shown great promise for your brother to place him in my path. Your brother never could bear to have anyone who could challenge him around." Sneering with a meaningful glance at her, "Perhaps even you? But now he belongs to me. Don't you Boyo?"

Boyo's quick response could be said to have adoration or perhaps only sheer fear laced through his voice, even as he speaks, "Oh yes Mistress this slave lives to kneel before you." I smile to reward him.

Leaning down to her face I almost whisper in her ear, "You see my dear you cannot win. Nothing or no one can or will save you. Think back in all your time in London and in Hell, have you ever heard of an Inq saving anyone? Did that ever happen? No! So now you are lost, soon to be dammed by even your own kind."

Face up with her head and shoulder supported by Boyo, stretching her out so that her head is raised but still lower than her hips I can now stand behind her and watch her reactions as I begin to once again stroke her clit, this time not with my talons but the tip of my finger. She is sobbing from the pain in her arms with her eyes closed to try and block out some of the agony but with that single touch her eyes fly open wide in terror.

Realizing my intent is to cause her arousal she tries to struggle against Boyo and begs, "No please don't do that to me now! Please! Haven't you already done enough?"

Laughing softly as I stroke her clit with one hand, while with the other hand I slowly slide a talon inside her. Her thighs are trembling and I feel her tighten around my finger as her urgency increases. She is openly crying now, tears cutting trails down her cheeks as she moves her head from side to side in denial of her need. Her spelled lust is combining with her pain and she can't help herself.

There is no way that she knows of the spell I cast but just as her body reaches for a shuddering and shattering climax, I lower my lips to her and suck her clit, my forked tongue lashing like a whip takes her over the edge. Her orgasm is extended by my licking and flicking but shortly after I lower the chains that hold her hooves in the air. Her legs are still spread wide apart but now she has a cold stone floor to lie on, voraciously I climb through her legs, licking, nibbling and nipping my way up her body until I reach her lips. She tries to look away but she is held by Boyo at the shoulders and I clasp her head firmly in my hands grabbing her on either side of her face. I look into her eyes just inches from my own and murmur, "You can't help yourself now. Others of your kind will have given you up, you're helpless against me. You cannot even hope to be held by me and not cum screaming." Then I lower my mouth to her unwilling lips and kiss her as gently and as tentatively as if it was the first kiss I ever gave.

As I raise my mouth from her lips I rejoice in seeing her closed eyes and the tears starting again. I whisper into her ear gently, "You knew this would be your fate when you surrendered to me and soon you will surrender your whole self to me. Day by day you shall lose more and more of your former self as I strip your morals from you, until you lose the link to your cult's magic and your brother can no longer summon you." I can see my enemy weaken, she is moaning and panting now aroused not only by the spell but the very essence of my being and the heady aroma that only a Succi demoness can produce. When she begins to spasm, as her eyes glaze over I hold her in my arms praising her for her howls making sure she knows how helpless she is against the true power of a Succi.

The helplessness that she is feeling, the vulnerability of being controlled completely by another is what I need her to understand. Finally when she is truly exhausted not even having the strength to raise her head, I rise and nod to Boyo who helps me to chain her to the wall. She is crying without shame or perhaps from shame but sobbing her heart out none the less. This I take as a good thing and snap my fingers before pointing to a carafe of blood red beverage. Boyo leaps to appease me, carefully pouring the ruby red Claret into a stemmed glass. Moving to her once more I take a sip while stroking her head then lean over to kiss her. This time there is no resistance, her lips part for mine and I let a small trickle of wine seep between us. I smile at her before speaking, my voice surprising myself, even to me it sounds deeper cloaked in an almost palpable smoky passion. "I could become fond of you in spite of all your transgressions against us and having to kill you every day then chase you down and bring you back is a chore I don't really relish. Believe it or not we Succi's have far nicer things to do with others; it is mainly the Inq's that like to kill."

I see it then that first faintest glimmer of hope in her eyes; I take another sip this time fully sharing it with her. "I cannot allow your brother to summon you ever again! You must understand that before all else. If you are ever summoned again, my Mistress and my sisters would be at risk. I cannot let that happen but there is another way. I will have to kill you at least several more times, sadly, this cannot be helped but if I can lower your morals enough, you will no longer have your powers or even be a true Inq. So my Boyo and I are going to cleanse you of your holier thanthou nature. I can see glimmerings of hope in that direction already."

There is near panic in her eyes as she shakes her head in denial. Her face flushes as she chokes out the words, "Please no, not that! I'll take any vow never to harm your family, I'll do whatever you ask or command but please don't take my magic from me!"

She is afraid now, not of pain, not of being killed or harried from plane to plane, she is afraid of having her beliefs and power torn from her mind. I place my middle finger over the center of her lips pressing gently. "This is my will. I'll strip you naked from the inside out but fear not for I will also fill you with that which I prefer, what you want, what you beg for is of no consequence here. That passed when you surrendered to me." Moving close to her ear, I raise the glass to her lips letting her sip before I whisper, "And your powers my prisoner shall never return."

I have her now and she knows it, I am quite sure that if she feared me while I plagued her through the hells, she is now in utter terror of me. As a final gesture before leaving her with her thoughts, I lean forward to kiss her thoroughly once more using my forked tongue to explore, twisting and capturing around her own deep in her mouth. This time she tenses as if I had attacked her but this time she does not, cannot turn away from my kiss.

Satisfied I turn to Boyo, "Come MINE you have done well this day." He runs to me, now I see no fear in his eyes only his need to please. I bring him directly in front of the demoness Macey and then take him by the collar forcing him look at her. "Would you enjoy having her now as your reward MINE?" I look at them both knowing full well of their previous alliance, her looking at him with revulsion and sheer horror but as he looks at her, his eyes pull away and he turns back to stare at my feet.

"Your slave only serves to please and entertain you as you wish Mistress; your desire is his command."

"Then my sweet sausage take her in your arms, kiss her, stroke her even hold her gently while I am gone. I want you to arouse her fully and continually but do not enter her even if, no! Especially if she begs you to but rather apologized nicely telling her that later your Mistress will let you pleasure her." With that I turn to leave having total confidence that Boyo will do exactly as I instructed. I stride up the stairs to have a momentary bit of privacy and take out my Hell-phone texting Mistress that Macey will be well taken care of for the foreseeable future.

Returning to my dungeon, I allow myself a minute to just enjoy watching Macey trying to pull away from Boyo who is holding her in his arms and kissing her throat and breasts. She is looking away and he is intent upon a nipple while silently I slip up behind him. Reaching forward one hand going low to trap his almost hard cock while the other glides high to his collar; I pull him back into me, forcing him to release Macey. Breathing heavily into his ear, "You have done well today MINE; you have shown me you can be a good Boyo." Deliberately letting my tongue slide over the side of his neck, my tail wraps itself twisting upward around his leg to tease his balls. Still holding hard to his cock, I hear him moan slightly. He is relaxing in my arms, while his cock becomes harder in my grip. Releasing my tail I turn him towards me, holding his rod harder now with a pulsing grip, pulling him tight against me as I lift one leg and wrap it behind the small of his back. Boyo and I are scant inches in front of Macey, close enough for my aroma to more than arouse her even though she looks on in a shocked horrified trance. This is perfect I wriggle my tail tip sliding it up her leg as I kiss Boyo deeply on the lips and rub myself on his rock hard member.

My tail reaches higher on her sliding up her inner thighs. She tries to move away but is tightly chained to the wall by her ankles and wrists and can get no leverage at all. Boyo has leverage now as I raise myself on tip toes and slowly cover his cock with me, my tail tip presses hard into Macey searching for her passion spot. I hear her curse me but then moan no longer able to control her arousal. Boyo lifts me up and down sliding me easily on his cock, causing my muscles to contract and release around his manhood. My own arousal peaks hard and perfectly in time with not only Boyo but with Macey as well, who's shuddering climax causes her to scream my name.

Chapter Nine

My mouth goes dry as I realize that my foot would have gone right through the floor just as easily as my hand did. Gritting my teeth and fighting off the fear I press my hand down feeling for something beneath the floor that is not there. Feeling nothing I softly call out, "Hex sister, please help me!" She is by my side in an instant and sees the trap before us. Inspecting it carefully as Mistress comes up to join us she motions the rest of the party back.

"Mistress this is like the wall leading to our ritual room, I can make it solid at least for a time but it would be better to see what is on the other side of this illusion." Hex turns to Mistress continuing, "This draft is cold and dank and it may hide other passages or even a device to activate the trap when we are half way across, someone should go through the floor preferably on a rope."

The consideration on Mistress's face is so evident that I don't even have to feel her concern about splitting the party but see her relent and whisper back, "Cyril borrow some of Sugar's silk rope you would be the best person here for this because Sugar could not call up to us to tell us what is happening." Sugar quickly slips a coil of thin rope from her pack and begins to fashion a double sling with four loops formed by two knots.

Cyril takes a quick back step, "Look I appreciate being here and all but I'm not the heroic type. I avoid trouble; I don't have armor or great big swords or even a wand. I think you're making a mistake here, I just don't do things like lower myself into what we know is a trap." He takes one more step back almost as if he is going to run but finds himself in front of Slice, who merely reaches down to Cyril's crotch and pats it gently. Having effectively communicated his message Slice shoves him forward to Sugar. Cyril turns a grey color and has the look of a man stepping up to the gallows as Sugar takes him by the hand.

"My body is not really doing this; I'm really running back down the tunnel to safety. Really, what you see here is just an illusion so why not just ignore it?" His voice has a panicky edge to it as his eyes dart from face to face of those around him.

But Sugar just places her hand on her throat and a finger on his lips calmly saying, "A wise assassin is a quiet one. You are just going to climb down a wall and look around, just take it one careful step at a time and it will be fine." The pain is evident to everyone that her squeaky whisper has caused her. Seeing this Cyril stands a bit taller, solemnly closes his eyes and then in resignation nods.

Sugar now satisfied her efforts have not been in vain arranges her knots with one loop each for his legs and arms, before passing the line to Slice. Holding her throat with one hand and speaking very softly so her voice does not squeak as much, she whispers to both, "Don't let go Sir unless you feel three pulls, if you feel two then bring our friend up fast, but if you feel only one pull, hold the rope still." Turning Cyril to face her and not the trap she reaches up to touch his face gently before he tentatively lowers his heels letting them sink into the trapped floor and begins to walk backwards down the wall. Bracing his feet against the side he cautiously lowers himself and disappears beneath the fake stone.

Shivering when I see Cyril's head go below the floor and almost holding my breath in fear, I realize even through my gauntlets that my grip is too tight on my wand. I force myself to lose n my hand in case I squeeze the turning too tightly and fire by mistake. After a wait that seems unending we make out the whispered words hollowly coming from some distance away as if he is in a large empty place.

"It's deep, more than 30 feet and it is probably 50 feet long. There are sharpened stakes here with a lot of bones." Pausing to for a minute he continues, "But this seems to be the end of a large cavern with a whole lot of water and even some old boats. There are some rusty weapons and the remains of armor that is old and useless. There are also some stair steps as if this was once the passage itself but they lead to a spot on either side where the landing has been removed. I don't see anything else that would be a threat down here but give me a minute I want to check some bodies."

We stand there waiting not all that patiently but after another short pause I see the jerk on the rope indicating that he wants up.

As Mistress Copper turns to Hex I can sense curiosity, "Hex, have any of your researches led you to any references of something like a great underground lake that needs boats? I must say I'm more than a little interested it is almost a shame we have a quest and a war to deal with first." But with a quick wink and charming smile, beams at Dovey, "What say you my pink frocked friend, shall we later delve these depths?"

"Pink! Pink? Definitely not pink, it is FAA-YOU-SHA!" Dovey loudly avers with a completely straight face. "And you could not keep me away with a dozen of Sugar's silk ropes," glancing to the side, with a wanton leer and a wayward wink at Cum, she chuckles, "But I know who could try."

With Slice pulling the rope Cyril's hooded head soon rises almost magically through the floor. After he unfastens himself and Sugar recoils her silk ropes, he takes a small book from his pouch and hands it Mistress saying, "I found this clutched in one of the skeletal hands. I knew it would be way out of my league so didn't even try to open it." He goes to hand it to Mistress but Hex intercepts it whispering, "These old books can sometimes have traps for the unwary that is after all part of what happened to me when I lost my hair."

Hex first intones a word of power and after finding no magic hands the book to Sugar who quickly picks the lock. Mistress Copper takes the book from Sugar.

"This appears to be a diary or log book, it is very old and the writing has faded but it appears to be a history of a band of men called 'The Last Heroes'. Later perhaps Hex, you would care to research this as we have scant history of our world." Handing the book to Hex Mistress turns to ruffle Cyril's hair. "You have the instincts of a thief Lad, if there is ever anything of value you will always be the first to find it."

Hex turning to the challenge of the trap takes out her ornately jeweled silver dagger and after first kissing the blade, sending a tremble up my inner thigh, holds it to the surface of the floor and breaths a word of power. Stooping as she holds the dagger in place she raps the butt of her wand on the now solid floor and indicates for to me to continue.

Feeling no great desire to fall through the floor, I take great care to emulate Hex's trick with my wand, gently tapping about once every pace. We continue in this manner, me tap, tap, tapping away, followed by Slice and Hex, Mistress is close behind Sugar and Cyril with the rest of our party spread out behind. For my part it is now grueling work, with every step there is risk but for every step I safely take we are closer to our destination.

I never know where that trap left off but I kept on checking the floor with my wand until after many hours Mistress finally calls a halt for a rest and a bite to eat. When she calls to me I gratefully kneel before her, every part of my body screaming from tension. Mistress sits on her pack stroking my hair before feeding me some of my chopped carrots and dried meat. "You have done well MINE, you have saved us once today already so rest here at my feet for a bit before we continue and I'll enhance you when we start. I can feel how much this is taking out of you but I am so very proud of you."

We all eat and drink the water we have with us. We all rest except Hex who seems to devour the book Sugar found, treating it like a fine feast while she absently munches on that which is inconsequential. From time to time she looks up and frowns as if puzzled by some reference or merely trying to catalogue some obscure factoid. But when Mistress signals us to rise, she goes to Mistress and I can hear her say, "This book is from a time we have no history of and speaks of things that make this reader believe there is much more to understand than ever before. This book is a treasure of knowledge that's been lost for generations; this knowledge whether lost or perhaps stolen must reach the upper world and be shared with others."

Mistress merely looks at Hex saying, "Later MINE, we focus first on the knife at our throats not the spears in the distance!"

Having eaten and rested, also having had a spell cast on me to give me more strength I set off in the lead once more, still tapping. This time our journey seems easier not only do I have twice the strength and awareness that I had before but Mistress's mind is more at ease, she now sees us functioning well. That reassurance is what I need to be able to use my mind to feel ahead of us. Until finally I have another glimmering of something just not quite right ahead.

I stop dead! I know that this is not a mere trap; I have exactly the same feeling of a malevolent force watching our every move that I had experienced from that dead bird. I motion everyone back far enough until there was no trace of the feeling then talking in whispers I tell Mistress and Hex the problem. I have faith that Mistress will know the answer but it is Hex that looks at the book and whispers, "Those who died in the pit had believed they were being spied on in these tunnels long ago. They spoke of this spying as done by devices not living things."

Mistress looking at me instructs, "You destroyed them once, do so again MINE, this time quickly and completely, we must not let these things hamper us. So go quickly."

With that I turn and run into the blackness toward the source of the feeling. There, I know it! I move closer whirl and fire once, twice, five times in all before the feeling dies. Hex and Slice lead the rest forward to where I stand panting, not from exertion but from the sheer exhilaration of utterly destroying a menace. There is a gaping crater that has been gouged out of the wall by the force of my repeated blasts, when the lanterns are shone in the newly formed cavity we see a tunnel that leads away into the darkness and the scorched shards of a once golden device with tiny splinters of glass strewn around.

Mistress looks at Dovey who just shrugs, saying, "I really don't know what this means but I will be back to take a look."

Mistress scratches her chin; I can feel emotions warring within her, the desire to explore and the need to finish the quest. "Mysteries within mysteries, we are going to get to the bottom of this but not today." Turning to Hex Mistress asks, "How much further to our goal MINE?"

"The old texts said it was a nine hour walk and we have been going for almost ten so it has to be close Mistress."

But somehow her words do not seem to ring true to me for shortly after, the path began to slope down. I am very aware of my surroundings, concentrating on even the slightest differences. The drop may not have been noticed by everyone or even that the air seems to have become poorer somehow heavier and less wholesome but we proceed on down for a short while longer until the floor abruptly levels out and the lanterns illuminate a heavy old rusty iron grate in the tunnel wall to our left. Peering through the barrier, we can see that not far from our position the roof has come down filling into the passage, beside us in the direction we have been traveling is a sheer faced wall.

It seems to me our journey has been in vain, for we are very deep underground now and even if we could get past the grating we have no hope of digging out the passage. But it is Cyril who wanders up to the wall face and maybe in frustration slaps it with his gloved hand. A puzzled expression spread over his face and putting a finger to his lips motions Mistress forward.

Mistress in a hushed voice calls for all of us to come forward and says, "This wall is another hollow illusion. I'm going to try the same spell we use on our wall to go to the 'Altars' but everyone have their weapons at the ready."

As a group we rapidly deploy, Dovey is in the center wand out with her terrible tutu all unfolded. Flanked by Slice, one huge sword in his right hand and a smaller three bladed dagger in his left, and Cum with sword, shield and a lethal grin, a grin shared surprisingly by Taken, just behind his right shoulder. Mistress Copper positions herself behind holding her whip at ready with Sugar watching her back. The rest of us are scattered where we can fit, waiting for a target. We stand at the ready as Hex casts strengthening spells on all of us so fast, I see her almost stagger. But it is Mistress who

94

reaches over Dovey's head and raps the wall with her dagger, intoning a word then quickly steps back with whip in hand.

Mistress looks to me quizzically and I reach out with my mind feeling ahead, sensing nothing I shake my head, and hear Mistress say loudly, "CHARGE!" We as one dash through the wall coming to the first corner we have encountered in a whole day's march. As a unit we turn the corner in a rush prepared to blast anyone offering resistance to dust. But we have only come to an empty room. Well not really empty for when we shine the lanterns around we see a large room and at the center a spiral staircase going up. While there are no visible threats that I can see or 'feel', the stairs leading up are very narrow and that will force our party to go up in single file. However shining the lanterns around further we become aware that the walls are lined with a vast array of devices all similar and all very large but surprisingly they appear to have the same gold and ceramic surface as we found in the nightingale and in the blasted wall. But these devices seem dead to me. They hold no threats or feelings that I can detect; they resemble nothing more or less than a normal simple machine. I am sure there is a reason for these being here but what it was I have no idea but they do not hold the same taint of active malice that the others had. There is also a heavy closed door off to one side of the room.

After our fearless charge everyone seems slightly let down except for perhaps Dovey, who stands there like a small mountain or a large cup cake with pink, sorry '**Faa-you-sha**' icing, her brightly painted Tutu still sticking out from her waist like a pink porcupine with a Navaho cut, growling about grizzly ghosts that need gutting, as she scuffs her shoes on the floor. The other notable exception is Hex who glides over to the devices like someone enraptured and perhaps she is. Her hands hover over what appears to be controls for the devices; she is intently studying everything about them, going first to one then another then back to the first like a person unable to choose a candy. Slice, Cum and myself go to the stairs and I begin checking for traps, while both Sugar and Cyril examine the door together. I can see no hidden threats from the stairway so move to Sugar and Cyril at the door. They both are running their fingers over the hinges and lock and as I move closer I notice the furtive glances they exchange as they examine the door.

Finally it is Cyril that steps back saying, "There is no trace of a trap here and this lock will pop like a plum when I pick it."

Mistress nods and responds, "We had better at least see what is behind the door, I don't like all these machines here and even the chance of an ambush is not something we need." With wands out and blades drawn, all standing behind Cyril he bends to his task. The thief has not lied, for that matter he even gets an appreciative nod from Sugar as his pick quickly and unerringly opens the lock. Taking his position on the hinged side of the door, he steps back and pulls open the heavy metal door. Not a squeak or a single groan comes from those well-oiled hinges. On opening, there is another passage which smells and looks not only dust free and clean but actually tiled and well used.

"You had better put an alarm on that door Cyril lad but I must say you know how to use your picks." With that Mistress turns to the stairs saying, "I suppose we should see what is upstairs as well, so come on let's do this thing and then we can set up a camp."

Mistress points to me to lead and up I go feeling, seeing, touching my way around and around the stairs, seven times I rotate around that central post always moving up the steep steps. After the first few steps the dust on the treads of the step increases and I am able to tell that no boot has trod here recently. I continue until I reach the last step and a small landing with a ladder going up to a stone ceiling with a lever on the wall. With Slice and Hex beside me on the landing and Mistress Copper on the top step she silently motioned for me to pull the leaver. There was an instant of silence followed by the rasping sound of stone moving over stone.

The ceiling rises above me and looking up I can see stars in the sky. Hearing the sound of surprised voices I know that someone is up above. Rushing up the ladder as much to clear the way for the others as anything, I see before me perhaps thirty of the beastlings that normally attack but this time they are all on their knees in front of me. Jumping to the side I have my wand ready but do not fire. Hex and Slice are out only half a breath behind me and join me at the side. The scene in front of us does not change and Hex actually places her hand on Slice's arm saying, "Wait we need to understand this." As one by one each emerge from the passageway and spread out keeping all weapons ready until finally everyone is standing with their back to a stone altar that has been raised exposing the opening we have just come out of. Surrounded by beastlings on their knees chanting words I do not understand is not a comfortable experience. We look around and see that outside them are huge stones in a ring, many in pairs with another stone resting on the top.

Stepping forward Hex speaks loudly, "We ask for information about the Skelton King?"

In response a single truly ugly beastling stands saying, "What you seek is not ours to give, for he is hidden. Perhaps the Succi Goddess Lillith may offer you more of a location. But I can say this; you will need to steal a candle from her and another from the Inquisitor God. Take those with a Crystal Chalice and a Golden Bell to meet with the Skeleton King. You are seekers after old lore so we leave you now in peace." With that pronouncement all of the beastlings including the speaker silently rise and leave us in the ring of ancient stones.

We still stand in high alert while Mistress walks around the circle seeking out any dangers but on returning says, "We camp here for the night. Everyone will pair off with one other and each pair will stand guard for two hours. Crap love can you figure out a way to get that altar back the way it was? We don't want to have to defend from both the inside and the out. Cyril and Taken you take first watch. Now let's eat and get some sleep. I don't suppose tomorrow will be any easier than today."

We wearily eat and wash it down with nearly the last of our water and then quickly choose shifts. Snuggling up behind an already sleeping Mistress with every intention of just keeping her back from getting cold, I let my eyes close for just a moment. The next I thing I know Toy is quietly shaking my arm for my turn at guard duty. I move quietly away from Mistress walking between couples and trios hearing their soft murmurs, little sighs and ungentle snores.

Seeing Crap and Slice finish their shift then bed down together, we take a careful look around working on the task of remaining alert. Toy and I prowl just outside the stone rings taking note of the small alarms set by the others: a thin layer of dried twigs on a path, a branch left stretching across another path that will snap back into place if disturbed and lose round stones that will be treacherous to stand or step on carefully placed where someone would stand to spy on our party.

But while we prowl Toy starts a quiet conversation, "Doll, have you cast any spells yet? I'm sure your morals must be low enough for you to try."

"Sister having spells cast on a person does not teach her how to cast." Is my honest reply to her query. "If this slave knew how to cast she might have but her spell book is empty."

Toy looks around and takes out her own spell book opening it to the first page. "Look at this spell in my book sister; it is the spell of seduction. You need only to focus your mind on the spell, see the mystic writing in your mind's eye then find the word before you gesture to release it on your target."

Not really understanding what my sister is saying I look and concentrate, to my surprise I do see the symbols in my mind. I look up at Toy and instead of thanking her, a low moan slips from my lips as I draw one hand up my belly to my breast in a salacious gesture. From deep inside my mind I feel the spell release like a wave of heat passing from me to Toy. My body is drained the energy traveling to Toy. She looks at me in adoration as she slips to her knees in supplication.

Shocked I stagger back only to be followed by Toy on her knees. This is not right Mistress set us as guards; we have to guard the rest. I Look at Toy sternly saying, "Get up silly! Mistress told us to guard, playtime will be later." It seems to work as Toy at least starts to look around so I press again, "Now sister! Stand up now! You have to look for intruders." Toy complies with my suggestion immediately even though she kept looking back at me pleadingly. Our watch goes smoothly after that, although I do have to redirect Toy several more times. We finally end our watch in a similar manner to beginning it by checking the telltales and alarms. It is Mistress and Sugar who take the next watch. I can see how sorry Toy is when Mistress tells us to get some sleep because we will need it rather than enjoy the playtime she desires. But sheer exhaustion rules and neither of us presses the matter. The casting of the spell has taken a lot more out of me, more than I had thought; it is not a normal sort of tiredness but almost like an empty hole has been created by pouring out something from deep inside. Toy is not quite playful but very cuddly and clinging. I know then that when I do manage to sleep I certainly will not have to worry about getting cold.

Chapter Ten

In Hell Macey shivers in the dungeon of Spite; she is bound hand and hoof with chains she cannot break, lying on the floor. The powers of speech, smell and sight have been taken from her and even her hearing is severely limited by a hood over her head. The studded ball gag is more of a goad than a silencer but she knows all these are only the smallest part of her problems. She has been taken! She is a captive of a noble hellion. A Succi Princess, who just happens to be the 'Branded First Girl' of her brother's sworn enemy. She should have been prepared for the first attack which she has to acknowledge was her error but that would have meant asking someone else for help. The second error or problem was even worse. She had found she could not help but to keep erupting into some of the greatest orgasms of her very long life. The smell of her captor was enough to drive her further and further into these lecherous longings. Disgusted with herself almost more than if she was laying in filth, she stiffens as a finger traces over her throat.

I can see her startle at my touch and shake her head as I place a spiked choke chain around her throat. Holding the chain close to her throat I first gently, then with authority and finally cruelly pull to lead her out of the slave pen on her hands and knees. She moves grudgingly for me by placing her bound hands on the floor in front of her then pushing forward with her legs.

Her movements are awkward as her wrists are chained together in front leaving her bare knees as the principle method of moving forward. Leading her to the center of the room I whisper to Boyo to take off the hood I had placed on her last night. Boyo had been given explicit instructions of all the things he must do, can do and must not do, in this I had made certain that all was prepared for her. I want to be the first thing she sees so I stand directly in front of her and smile in my most menacing manner as Boyo unties and removes the hood from her head.

"Well how is the captive today? I trust your rest was not all that comfortable? But don't worry I assure you that you will learn to love that minor discomfort." As I turn and take out my trident I see her eyes widen. "That self-righteous brother of yours may try to summon you today. You must understand me now! That cannot and will not be allowed to happen so I'll just have to kill you later. The only question is whether it is swiftly done or as painfully as I can make it." Snapping the chain hard and seeing the barb bite into her throat, "You have violated someone so very dear to me that my inclination is to slowly tear you piece from piece. But perhaps if your behavior is appropriate I could be a bit gentler. Would you like that?"

I know very well that she knows of at least as many ways of causing pain as I do and has to be truly aware of what she faces. I let her think it through before removing her ball gag. "Well? Will you do as you are told? Or shall I slowly rip your to pieces? Your choice my dear, your choice alone, for in this you must decide?" I can almost see the tears form in her eyes with her certainty of my intentions increasing. But I see more than just her suspicions increase as I grab her hair and force her to a kneeling position. Her nipples have hardened and her nostrils are flared as my aroma starts to arouse her once more.

There is terror in her eyes when she looks at me. "Please I beg you, what must I do? I don't need any more of your lustful torture. I have surrendered to you completely, vowed never to attack your family, what more can you want. I am now your prisoner what more can you wish from me?"

Turning my back to her, "You're not stupid girl but you must think you're so very special for me to have to waste my time killing you every day, for all eternity." Then whirling I go back and grab her hair shouting, "What do you think I want? I want your morals gone fool, so you can never be summoned by your brother again. I want to drain those high and mighty, oh so holy Inquisitor morals out of you!"

The shock of realization is evident on her face and I feel her tremble in my grip, finally the recognition that she cannot stop me and that no matter what she does she is in my power. But even worse is the choice we both know she must make. To surrender all she believes in, or have me tear it out of her one atom of pain at a time.

Looking up at me she defiantly responds, "You have no more choice than I, except normally pain is my province not yours. That is why you are making this offer. You don't want to hurt me, your anger is waning and you really will make this as easy on me as you can."

But my proximity to her is now arousing her quickly. Her nipples are hard and her thighs trembling, even the line of her mouth is softening. Still I see the resolve harden in her face; she tries to struggle to her hooves to look me in the eye. Failing this, giving in to her mounting passions, she sadly lowers her head and in a defeated tone acknowledges, "I should not, it breaks everything I know but I have surrendered; I will try not to struggle or resist as you change me." Shuddering partly in rapidly increasing passion and with a small moan she implores, "Use me please, I just can't help myself."

I take her face in my hands and raise her lips to mine, kissing her tenderly before turning to Boyo. "The captive has made the proper choice MINE. I do not want her to regret her choice. Bring us food, wine and fragrant oils and the silks." I don't know if Macey has ever been properly used before but she has taken the first step and I have six hours left before I must kills her again. If I really try very hard she may even be able to lose enough morals so that her brother can no longer ever summon her. Studying her, it is obvious that she is now almost ready to explode but she is still trying to hold on to her illusions of purity and goodness even though no one can resist the arousal caused by my Succi demoness pheromones. Stepping forward I take a chain from overhead and hook it to the chains on her wrists. Whispering encouragingly, "I will help you to let go." I take my riding crop and raise a welt on her ass. "Do you feel that slut? Do you want to cum like a common back alley slut? Tell me how much you want it slut?" Smiling while I step away, I prevent her from using my aroma and pheromones to find release.

"I need it now please, I beg you. I'm on fire please! Please use me anyway you prefer, just please let me cum."

I laugh as Boyo passes me a glass of wine and a haunch of demon meat to gnaw on. Using the most imperious gesture and sadistic smile I can muster I point to her saying, "Boyo why don't you give our guest some food and drink she has been panting and moaning so; I'm quite sure her mouth must feel parched." I want her drowning in her own sensations for that reason I had chosen the most aromatic of demonic meat and wines I could find and my efforts are rewarded with the look of pleading on her face gradually becoming confused as she smells the wine and tastes the food. Of course she has to be ravenously hungry, I know that she had not gained any souls in London and I killed her repeatedly yesterday. Every time she woke on a different plane her hunger would have increased until now. I am rewarded by seeing her attacked the haunch of Demon meat tearing gobbets of it from the bone Boyo was holding, the raw fluids streaming down her cheeks. I give her exactly three swallows before he takes it away and I move close again.

Standing in front of her, so close that I am almost touching her, I wait and watch carefully to see her breathe three times before I lean even closer and brush my lips over her cheek. Now moving around behind her, reaching to grasp her nipple from behind I whisper in her ear, "Maybe I'll let you cum this time but you have to show me how much you need it. You have to make it clear that you are beyond mere preference and now have real need that drives you." I speak softly right into her ear, letting my breath warm her face and throat. "Can you do that for me Macey? Can you let yourself go that much?"

With one hand I begin to tease her nipple ever so gently my right arm moves forward to bring the crop down between her legs in a playful swat. With that touch, almost like a release her hips buck forward, as her back arches pressing her shoulders into me. Tugging on her nipple with just a little bit more force than she uses to press it into my hand, I strike with the crop one more time before I wrap my arms around her forcing her to inhale my essence. I squeeze her until her breath is driven from her lungs and hold her with no air like that for a short while before releasing her and forcing her to breathe the air saturated with my lust incarnate deep into her lungs.

She erupts first with the briefest of moans then with a howl to the heavens she has forever forsaken. Shaking, shuddering, crying out her orgasm in total abandon, I know it has started now. She is wallowing in lust and pure sensation beyond and all desire for chastity. I keep holding her and occasionally urge her to greater heights with a nibble, smack or tweak designed to prevent her from ending the orgasm. On and on she goes seconds stretching into minutes, panting moaning and howling out her passion, as those minutes are lost to hours. It takes almost two hour for her first real cumming before she slumps spent in her chains; her full weight supported by the chains that bite into her. I step back as she unconsciously moans out her satisfaction.

"Now that was a long time cumming my dear and do you know what I think? I think with a little practice you could get rather good at that."

Walking away once more she sighs and smiles exhaustedly in response. I cast a spell on her, not a spell to arouse, seduce, strengthen or heal, but rather one to allow me to know if my efforts have begun to purge her of her repulsive morality. The spell quickly tells me that while her morals have fallen and that her will is not against me, there is still much more to do. I can tell she has recognized the spell and its use.

"I am trying!" She anxiously cries, "Please you really must see that I am abiding by my word to you."

Striding over to her I take her by the hair. "My spell tells me you are still the same revenging beast that wounded my sister. You say you're trying but let face facts; you don't have a huge open window to make a choice, let alone jump through. You are barely trying, just sucking up what I give you. No you are going to have to do far more than that." I reach up and free her hands from the chains, letting her drop to the floor. "Now prove what you say, crawl on your belly to my slave and beg him to whip and fuck you." Leaning over her with my whip in my hand I shout in her ear, "DO IT NOW!" Then slash my whip down over her back and shoulders.

I have taken great care to make my Boyo attractive, he has been bathed, his hair shorn and brushed and his face is now framed by a manicured goatee. He is dressed in light lose new clothes brightly colors and perfectly fitted. Even his hooves have been polished to a fine sheen. She looks up at him and freezes. I take that second to grab the choke chain at her throat and drag her over to him saying, "Now beg Bitch! Beg to be fucked like the slut you are."

I see her lower her head knowing that I am telling her to shame herself in a way no Inquisitor could tolerate but I hear the words she speaks, "Please Sir, fuck this slut, she needs you to use her."

Passing the leash to Boyo I say, "Do her hard, but make sure she cums screaming." Success! Turning I walk out the door and up the stairs for this time she will have to have her orgasm without the aid of my pheromones.

I only have about an hour or so before I need to make sure she cannot be summoned today, but that will give me the time I need to get a phone for Boyo. He has been most helpful and has slipped into being my slave with an ease I find extremely satisfying, so his reward must be dealt with promptly. The task I had set him, to assist in lowering Macey's morals as fast as possible seems to be progressing well. This very exercise is almost a blessing in disguise as every time he helps me in this his own morals fall just as his bond with me increases. At this point he is much stronger than her so I do not have to worry about her escaping. I plan to travel to Armageddon to seek out a vendor and buy a couple of phones before checking to see how the two have proceeded.

Upon returning I am not disappointed to see he is just finishing his assigned task. Motioning for him to come to me I first reward him with a deep kiss, holding his face in both my hands. Breaking the kiss and with a side glance to Macey I take out the Hell-Phone and place it in his hand.

"MINE I have set the speed dial to get me as: Oh! Oh! One! The second the only other number is Oh! Oh! Two! This is the private number of Mistress Copper and is only to be used in the direst of needs. This is for you to keep; you must guard it carefully as both of those numbers are very private. I am going to trust you with this so do not let me down."

Walking over to Macey I take her by the leash but use my hand under her chin to make her stand. Sighing before I speak, "You too have done well but not well enough, so this must be done." I turn her quickly and stab her only once cleanly through the heart causing her to drop lifeless to the floor. Concentrating I realize she is in Elysium. Casting takes but a second as I transport myself there and run to trap her once more. This time when she sees me coming she does not flee but drops to her knees acknowledging the inevitable.

"I knew you would find me quickly. I will not run from you. I do acknowledge you as my captor." She then lowers her head and sobs out despondently, "I can't go back home now, my companions there would shun me. I have been changed so much that I would be caught between the two cults, belonging to neither. This is what you have done to me."

Chiding her gently, "You really could not expect differently, now could you? Perhaps you did not believe I was still loyal to Mistress, but my bond with her is still intact, forged from both lust and love, the love not even your brother could steal." As I raise her up to her feet preparing to cast and fly between planes again, I look into her eyes seeing neither the hate I expected nor the fear I had intended but rather she looks at me with an almost puzzled expression. She looks at me as if she is now torn between surrender or flight for her resistance has faded. "We must go!" I cast and we reappear near my door. Compelling her to her knees again, "This is a good time for you to learn your place now walk like a dog on all fours and if you're very good I might even give you a treat." With a smile I turn away from my door and head to the market by the most traveled route I can find, knowing the humiliation she will feel from being viewed by many as the pet of a Succi.

I walk very erect; Macey on all fours is at my left side for while the lead is in my right hand, the riding crop is in my left. I watch her carefully for the tiniest errors and when I see her miss a stride I swat her ass on her left cheek. She stumbles at the unexpected blow only to receive another on her right cheek. "Walk like a proper pet or I'll stripe your ass, now keep the pace up." Just to emphasis my command I swat her again this time much harder. Looking down I see not only that she is concentrating on pacing properly but that tears are beginning to run down her cheeks. Walking her through the market I meet and greet several other nobles but keep on walking, as far too often nobles compete at a very lethal level. But when I see small group men I come to a halt commanding not them but her. "Kneel before your betters slave!" Scrutinizing her sad attempt at kneeling, I lash her once across the shoulders. "You ignorant beast kneel properly, knees wide hooves together and expose to all what I have taken." Seeing her trying to comply is almost amusing but having started this it must be finished properly. Using my tail to push her knees almost straight out to the sides, I reach down and poke the handle of my whip into her ass, forcing her hips forward and exposing herself utterly to the six male Succi warriors she is being displayed for. Standing erect I ignore her whimpering and address the group directly. This 'Holy Hypocrite' could bring me trouble tonight so I ask you six to present yourselves to assist as guards. Your use of her will be your reward, are you in agreement?"

The highest ranked among them goes down on one knee to me and lowering his head, "Your wish is our command, two shall now accompany you while I lead the rest to your palace immediately and meet you there, Lady."

At a nod of my head he rises points to the three on our left and leaves rapidly. She glances up at me panic on her face; I can see her fear of serving the six. "You have a problem slut?" Is all I say but I smile and finger my whip as I see her skin become ashen at the horror and the realization of the depth of her captivity. I bend over and whispering into her ear, "You did not really understand did you? You are now my slave, taken in conquest and tonight you will learn that, with every opening in your body, over and over again. But I promised you a treat and a treat you shall have." It takes but a single breath of concentration for me to cast the arousal spell on her not once but twice. Smiling I see her hands fly to her breast and crotch as the first of a massive orgasm builds in her. Letting her, an Inquisitor Demoness cum howling in the center of the main Succi market place should amuse everyone here, as well as totally humiliate her.

Chapter Eleven

The rising sun that warms my cheek finally shines on my eyes to gently nudge me out of an untroubled sleep. I move Toy's head which is resting on my shoulder so I can rise without waking her. As I am hungry, I eat the mixture of grains and nuts from my pack washing it down with some cold filtered spring water someone had gathered the night before. Looking around I can see many of the family stirring even Cyril and Sugar who looked by their state of disarray to have had a very interesting night.

But I can feel Mistress just at the back of my mind looking at me puzzled and uneasy. I go to her and kneel, "How can your girl best serve you Mistress?"

Her response is short and curt, "What happened to you and Toy last night MINE?"

This was a thing I would have rather asked her about when she had more time but I answer quickly, "Your slave is not sure Mistress. When Toy asked if this girl had used any spells, she said that she did not know how. Toy opened her book and let this girl see the spell of seduction written there. The writing seemed to burn in my mind, it just rushed out of my mouth as I moaned and stroked myself. Toy was then obedient to your slave Mistress, but your slave does not really understand."

Mistress's response is very quick and not happy, she grabs my collar lifting me to my feet and backhanding me across the face. "You are a stupid little fool! Do you even realize what you have done? First, I rule this house; you and your sisters are MINE, all MINE and no one and I do mean no one comes between me and MINE, not even MINE. Casting that spell did exactly that. You shall be punished for that but that is not all. As a Succi, before you cast the leader of our cult, the Demigoddess Lillith must grant you the right to use those spells. That means that after I'm done punishing you, I'll have to present you to her, where she also will punish not only you but me as well for allowing it."

I feel a wave of heat, a hot cold horror rushes over me, stunned far more by her words than the hard slap on my face. I can feel her anger as she slams me back to the ground. I look up into her ignited eyes cringing before I drop my lips to her war sandals, kissing them through my choked sobs, "Please Mistress your slave begs that she takes this all. Let her have your punishment as well." I live to serve Mistress how could this horror have happened? That I have caused Mistress to be punished is unforgivable. By my own stupidity to have come between my sister and Mistress is so very wrong. I cannot hold back my tears or sobs but bitterly cry at the feet of Mistress.

"Crap, Cum take her, strip her then tie her to that tree to await my whip."

I am crying so hard I do not try resist, I barely feel them lifting me or even Crap taking my clothes off me. I am vaguely aware that they connect chains at my wrists and tie a rope around the chain before carrying me to a nearby tree. Cum throws the rope over a limb close to the tree but events are not really connecting in my mind. Instead, Mistress's feelings war inside my head with an intensity I have never realized could even exist before. Her anger at how foolish I have been mixed with guilt that she had not stopped me and real anguish at what she is going to have to do. I feel all her feelings rush and tumble over each other in confusion and pain. My own feelings painfully intense are soaked in utter shame, sodden with guilt and sinking into the horror of what I have done. All of this from both of us mixing, feeding and firing a blazing ball that is consuming both of us.

I am only barely aware when they pull me off my feet. Hanging suspended from the limb by just my wrists, Cum and Crap pass loops under my knees they tightly secure them around the tree. I hang by my wrists with my face, breasts, belly and thighs bound and pressing into the tree, my inner thighs and every ring and chain on me press hard by the merciless bark. I can only see the rough bark in front of my face and feel the coarseness chafing the front of my body. The bark catching on my rings is even more painful than the chains on my wrists, even my lips feel and taste the bark. Dimly in what is almost like a different lifetime I hear my loving Mistress's whip cut through the air before my back explodes in a coruscating crack of pain. I howl out a scream that seems to come all the way from my toes; but I also feel Mistress stagger as the whip strikes. I know she has felt the same burning pain. I can sense her anger is now mixed with the agony she is causing but I also sense her hard cold determination to do what must be done as the whip once more tears through my back. I try to shield her from my pain but the whip falls again and I feel her trying to take the pain from me even as her whip tears into my back driving my breasts into the rough bark. I scream to Mistress, "Punish ME! Whip ME! Punish THIS slave!" Begging her not to take the pain, the pain is mind numbing for me, but it is mine. The horror of Mistress feeling my pain staggers my mind, as again the whip lashes my back this time painfully forcing my entire front, my breast, my thighs and even my lips and clit onto the hard rough bark. Pain is all around me, from the whip, from the tree, from Mistress. White hot pain, pain I must protect Mistress from.

Biting down on the bark before me, trying to barricade myself from Mistress I thrust my hips into the tree driving the pain with it. I force the pain from between my thighs into the evil bark which tears at me. I press my breasts and thighs hard against the tree with all of my might and as the whip lashes my back pouring burning agony on me, I thrust my hips harder into the tree again driving the pain out into my enemy, the woody bark of the tree itself. I cannot feel Mistress only the pain and the tree. I hate this tree. I find the core of my pain, grappling it with my hips and pour it into the wooden core. Again and again the whip falls, it is just me and this hated tree each time the world withdraws a bit more leaving whiteness and pain in its stead until there is only white hot agony searing and consuming me. Then all goes black.

I wake on the forest floor without pain, naked with Mistress standing over me, bloody whip in hand. I have been healed, raising myself then lowering my head before Mistress, "Your slave has such sorrow Mistress, she feels such shame that she cannot even beg for forgiveness."

What I feel in Mistress now startles me more than even the whip, she is feeling both proud and puzzled as she whispers to me, "How did you block the pain from me MINE? I was feeling ever bite of the whip for four lashes then nothing. How did you do that?"

"The tree Mistress, I forced the pain into the tree. I dragged the pain from me and drove it into the tree so you would be free."

We both look to the tree and see that it has been stained with the blood not only from the whip wounds but also from the scrapes and abrasions to the front of my body as well. But we also see Cyril, standing with hands in motion, hands almost touching the tree appearing to stroke and caress, almost soothing where the blood had stained it. I look in askance at Mistress as she looks at me, shrugs and shakes her head, "Men, love them at your peril but never try to understand them. They are such fickle creatures. Now get dressed MINE, we are on a quest. I healed you so you could be more than dead weight and you had better make the spell worthwhile. We have to make Westminster by noon so hurry girl! You still have point duty today but Slice should know the way through the forest so follow his directions."

As we form up I realize I'm a lot happier to be going through a forest than underground in the tunnels. Slice has said it should take about two hours to hike to the Tower station from where we can then transport to Westminster. I start off at a fairly brisk pace, at least for the first half hour until Dovey starts to make mention of long legged louts who were almost blonde enough to step where angels fear to tread. I sort of think she might be referring to me or her brother Slice, so I slow up somewhat as Cyril is also complaining that rushing through the forest is a waste and should be a delight to be savored. We are ambushed only once by a gang of ten or so beastlings who die so fast no one has a chance to take more than two attacks. Despite the mutterings from Dovey and Cyril, all things are completed in about two and a half hours and we arrive.

Aware to any dangers, I make the jump through the green arrow to Westminster Station then stand back in a guard position as the rest arrive. Mistress Copper waves me back saying, "I lead from here but I still want you at my left and one step back."

With Mistress in the lead we once more climb the steps out of the station into the bright sunlight. A short way ahead of us lays the ruins of what once must have been a palatial temple. The remaining walls, spires and roofs show the effects of time with both major and minor damage visible but rather than an atmosphere of decay or desolation there are many people coming and going all seemingly on missions of the greatest of importance. This hustle and bustle creates a din in the air of men and women talking, some even shouting, as they walk, stroll or even run. As Mistress chooses our route I cannot help but notice the large number of those around us who smile, wave or nod in her direction. There are no hostile gazes, all are deferential but some are almost in adoration while others seem genuinely and pleasantly surprised to see her. Her feelings are the determination and commitment I know so well, she never even returns a greeting but carries on briskly much to a complaining Dovey's consternation.

We enter the huge building and travel from room to room without hesitation, many try to engage Mistress in conversation but she merely waves their attentions away. Onward we go deeper and deeper into the structure as we travel I noticed how the furnishings are becoming more and more luxurious but we move so quickly I have little or no time to examine them. Finally we reach a huge set of double doors set into a high arching frame carved from stone. In front of the door stands four heavily armored and armed guards as well as to one side a very old woman sitting at a desk.

Mistress turns to the elderly lady and nods to her smiling as she asks, "Will Lillith be available soon Madeline?"

A dry wispy breath of a reply comes from her, "Oh Felicity, you know better. She has been waiting for you, not all that patiently all morning. Now in you go quickly, step sharp now young lady."

Never had I imagined anyone speaking to mistress in such a manner, instinctively my hands tighten on my wand just as Mistress grabs my shoulder, "Shhhh MINE this is as it should be." She turns pushing me to walk in front of her by holding hard to my collar.

My, "Yes Mistress!" is quick and my actions to comply fast but for a moment I think I see a fleeting smile drift over the craggy face of the old crone at the desk. The guards not only give way but open the door for

Mistress and we enter a huge throne room.

There are pews to either side of a plush red carpet running from the door to a raised dais with a tall throne on it. On the throne is the figure of a woman seated, crowned and wrapped in a plush regal red robe trimmed with white ermine. No echo can be heard as all eleven of us walk along that endless carpet. As we approach the throne I began to feel a sense of awe, the splendor of the room, every ornate fixture, the plush carpet so soft under my feet seem overwhelm my senses by their majesty. The figure on the throne, a small but beautiful woman seems almost insignificant but I know that the awe Mistress is feeling is directed at her. But there is more than awe, anticipation and fear are there too. This revelation brings me back into focus; Mistress has called the figure Lillith and has referred to her as a Demigoddess. I falter a step but Mistress's firm hand on my collar steadies me and forces me on until I am made to kneel in front of the figure.

"Copper I see no scars on this one throat? The quest damn it girl! Who is the questor?"

I feel her eyes on me now, my very skin seems to itch and crawl in her relentless gaze.

"Ah now I see. This one of yours has sinned." There is a penalty for that, make her rise and come to me. Mistress pulls on my collar forcing me to rise and presses me forward releasing the collar from her grasp. I can feel the fear in Mistress now, it only matches my own. I can't help it but my knees start to weaken as I move before the throne. "Strip girl let me see you quickly now!"

I drop my armor as fast as I can until I see her raise her hand bidding me to stop. As she walks around me I shiver in fright. Not from the cool room, not from her gaze that makes my very skin want to crawl off my bones but from the sheer force of her person.

"Twenty one stripes from your snake whip Felicity and every one at full force which is barely appropriate for the sin of casting without permission; I will need to know the full story here."

Mistress answers hesitantly, I know she believes she must say this exactly right, "Doll has been mine for only a short time but has learned of servitude wonderfully. I have taken joy in everything she has done except this one transgression. In that I could find no malice or pride that governed her actions. Rather, her sister asked her about magic and only opened the book to show her what a spell looked like." Going closer Mistress almost whispers, "Toy had no way of knowing that when the brand was placed on my Doll other talents had woken. She has a bond that bridges my feelings to her and hers to me. Somehow in just seeing the written spell, her mind seized on it and it was cast. When I whipped her, I felt the first four blows as if I were her, that is how strong the bond has become, but then she somehow broke the bond forcing her pain into the tree." Mistress has kept her head bowed throughout the whole explanation speaking lowly and directly to the now pacing figure, who has drawneven nearer while Mistress whispers. I can detect a tiny victory in Mistress's mind over that.

Straitening up Lillith reaches out to take my chin in her hand and pulling my face closer, "Your book girl, go get it now!" Is the command to which I jump. After quickly turning and digging my book out of my pack I return to her only to find she has moved directly in front of me. "You have had enough punishment for now Doll, give me the book. You have the makings of a great if not perhaps even a high Succi as such this would normally be a festive occasion but your sin in casting without permission as well as the quest you are on must take precedence. The quest is one of highest possible importance and will impact many more than stand here today; you must hasten to this task." As I offer up my spell book to her I hear her pronouncement. "You are hereby given your first two spells 'Seduction' and

'Greater Healing'. You have become Succi! Every Succi must first be the healer, then the warrior and the temptress. The punishment for your sin, a punishment you so richly deserve shall come later."

I feel Mistress's pride. She is so proud of me, it feels wonderful I almost cry but suddenly I'm quashed by a wave of fear from Mistress as the Demigoddess comes down off the dais and walks toward Toy. Taking Toy by the collar she leads her back to the front of the throne, turns and addresses us all.

"Felicity Copper, High Succi, Mistress of the Whip, Heir to the House of Copper, for failure to prevent a sin among those you have leashed and led, you shall lose this slave until she has learned not to meddle in the affairs her Mistress must control."

I feel Mistress mentally reel as if hit by a hammer but the Demigoddess continued, "After I release this slave back to you she shall bear the red whip. Your slave Doll shall return with it to me and stay to be my acolyte until I have personally trained her." Mistress staggers backwards a step before she regains her composure and pulls me closer to her.

The Demigoddess Lillith returns to her dais and towers over us all, just by the force of her being alone then looking solemn merely taps her toe for attention and gestures to us all. "Sugar, slave of the Mistress of the Whip, High Assassin of Westminster and Greenwich, the candles you just stole are actually part of the quest you are on, I understand that but your restitution for the theft will be to get me detailed pictures of your Mistress's 'Lascivious wall'. I wish you all well on your quest, for it is far more desperate than you could know. Now all of you hasten to your task! "

As those words still echo among us she snaps a leash on Toy, turns, raises a hand and vanishes with Toy.

Mistress hurts but will not show it, she takes my collar firmly turns and leads me and the remaining eight from the room, retracing the path we entered by. She does not look left of right or even wave or nod to anybody. Not one of us even whispers but we all know Toy has been taken from us and later so will I.

Leaving the temple, Mistress is feeling even more concerned and when she sees my inquiring look she speaks to all of us. "There may be a problem here, Lillith took away Toy which is her right but the quest did specifically say that we need ten people along with the questor Sugar to complete it. We may have to go back and get Pepper after all, but first we should get the other set of candles from Oxford." Returning to the station we transfer to Oxford and leave the underground emerging into bright sunlight shining down on the ivy covered walls of an extensive complex of old buildings.

Everyone tenses as we see the number of armed people here, no Succi other than us is visible in the whole area. Men and woman heavily armored in the most concealing of clothing with the very sight of us brings weapons to every hand as it becomes eminently clear we are the intruders here. As guards close in from every side Mistress Copper merely raises her arm and speaking in a loud clear voice pronounces, "We are here not for violence but for a quest that bears no one ill. We request passage to Thomas." Fully twenty five guards with wands and swords surround us now but one wearing a gold cloak over pure white armor strides to the foreground.

He walks up to Mistress easily balanced on the balls of his feet with a sword almost as long as Slice's in his hand. "My name is Horatio, as Inquisitor General it is my job to keep this area secure, as such I will not let you proceed to the inner chamber bearing arms but will give an oath that if no violence or evil actions take place they will be returned to you on your departure." He then motions several men forward who carry chests long enough for a sword or a wand and wide enough for several weapons.

Mistress looks around then smiles directly at him before she says, "I said we were not here for violence but going unarmed into an enemy's hold is as much a leap of faith as jumping off a bridge. Yet our quest is so urgent I will agree on a single condition. My title as 'Mistress of the Whip' allows me to bear my whip anywhere, anytime, this is my right and I will not give up my whip under any circumstances but the rest of the party's weapons may stay here if you personally stay in range of my whip."

His own face creases into a smile as he says. "Done and done, and trust a Succi to get two conditions out of one. Jansen you shall not open that box after the weapons are place there, you will be responsible for the contents so make sure nothing is disturbed in our absence." With that he merely gestured to the first box where Mistress Copper carefully lays her silver dagger. I am next placing my wand in it before moving to stand between Mistress and the man. All of us have to place our weapons inside the boxes but really many of us still are dangerous, the spikes on my left arm could rake an enemy badly, Mistress has heels on her war sandals to kill with and Dovey's tutu can easily tear apart wood, let alone flesh and bone. The thought of Hex not having enough spell power to do damage is just plain silly but no one has come for a fight although the Inquisitors all around us seemed to be ready for one.

Horatio sheaths his sword after the weapons are stowed but it is Hex who steps forward, "Jansen's honor should not be in question, my spell will ensure nothing is done by others that will compromise his zeal." With that she concentrates, intones a word of power and uses her hands to trace around each of the boxes. "Now not even time its self could break the spell, our weapons are secure Mistress."

Horatio nods before turning to lead us into the buildings through an open arch into a courtyard behind it. Going on from that courtyard we are marched through a labyrinth of hallways, passages and rooms with double doors, the twists and turns all that seem to be designed to confuse. We end at a small doorway with a brass door and dull metal frame set into stone. Even I have to duck to go inside and that is following the over seized Horatio who almost bends over double. Giggling, I turn to Mistress indicating his shapely ass.

Mistress being less than impressed with the direction of my gaze and thoughts is more concerned with not hitting her own head than with what is going on in mine, probably a very good thing. But after going in through the narrow entrance we see four more guards standing in front of a craggy faced man with a long scar around his throat. Even though he is not seated on his throne but actually down at our level he seems to have a massive presence about him. He is taller than any man perhaps over seven feet in height and his shoulders are colossal but his legs seemed to be more like small trees. Standing perfectly still he looks at us carefully for several minutes as if communing with the unknown. Abruptly he breaks his silence with a deep rich and resonating voice, "Ah yes, the thieves that come to steal my candles no doubt in a quest for the illumination of the world. Well get on with it but before you go there is business we must culminate. Well? Who is going to take the candles?" Mistress just nods to Sugar who is now standing behind him magical cloak off with two candles in her hands.

"Right! Succi thieves do have their talents, make note of that Horatio. Just as you are High Succi Felicity, Horatio is High Inquisitor. He took that title from your old nemesis Malthus after his last debacles and he did it in honest combat. What you may not be aware of is that this quest has far greater effects than merely removing the scars from your slave's throat."

He continues in almost a lyrical fashion, "This quest was lost long ago and has waited many hundreds of years to occur. It will remove the scars fear not, although finding and dealing with the Skeleton King is a quite different matter altogether, but the effects of your quest will resonate and perhaps if you truly successful even change all of London. However I see that you are now shorthanded. That will simply not do." Calmly looking over our shoulders to Horatio, he addresses him directly saying "But not for long. All Succi's and all Inq's will be affected by this quest so Horatio shall accompany you in this if you intend to get those candles out of here alive." As he ends he smiles in such a cold cruel and calculating way I just shivered. The Inq paladin's mouth drops open in shock, Mistress's mind does a triple take and I even hear Dovey's teeth grind together.

The man called Horatio falls down on one knee before the Demigod of his cult and lowers his head saying, "How have I offended you Sire, all my life I have worked hard to be worthy but now you sentence me to walk with evil? I do not understand what crime I have committed."

The Demigod Thomas just scoffs saying, "You're the last one to start whining about carrying out an order and this thing must be done! I am commanding you as the Inquisitor General to do your duty or you too could find yourself in the challenge ring."

Addressing the rest of us, "The next leg of your journey shall take you to the dankest reaches of the catacombs and there in 'The Room of Five Doorways to Oblivion' you shall find a chest. In that chest is the Crystal Chalice of Light required by the quest. But with the Chalice are twelve crystal skulls. Horatio, you will bring back four with you when and if you return. The 'Mistress of the Whip' if she survives will give four more to her Demigoddess. Finally all good and willing someone will give the balance to the Skeleton King. Now all of you leave, you Succi's are going to make me lose my composure and that is never a good thing, so all of you, out!"

Sugar is first out the door but the rest of us crowd after, except for Mistress, who turns back and just stares at Thomas until everyone is through the door. But before backing completely out Mistress raised her whip handle to her lips, kissing it in the most salacious manner possible, saluting as she leaves the room. I knew her private moment of glee then, to have teased a Demigod and gotten away with it.

Chapter Twelve

Strolling out of the main market square I Zap the leashed girl again while pleadingly she looks up begging, "Please not again I just can't take it anymore."

I slash my riding crop across her shoulder blades before taking her by the hair and forcing her to look directly into my eyes, "First, from now on you will call me Mistress!" To emphasis this I slash at her again; "Second, you were not given permission to speak!" Then slashing a third time, "Third, I am the one who decides what you do, when you do it, where you do it, how you do it and with whom you do it! Do you understand me now slave?" There is obvious fear in her eyes as her resistance continues to crumble from my attacks. I can almost taste that victory is in my grasp and when I release her hair her head drops down. I very softly hear the words I have been waiting for, "Yes Mistress."

"I did not hear you slave!"

This time the words are choked out in a louder voice, "Yes Mistress."

She can't see my grin but I can see that her orgasm is mounting fast so I time my next demand until just before her body breaks into spasms of passion. "Say that again slave, so that all the world can hear! Say it loudly!"

An Assassin's Quest

She howls as she cums but plainly screams the words through her orgasm, "Yes Mistress your slave understands!"

After her first eruption I raise her panting mouth to mine and brush my lips across hers before reassuring her, "I'll reward you for that later slave you are beginning to learn your place." Then reaching into my pouch I take out a ball gag, squeeze her throat until she opens her mouth then press and buckle it in place. "Now this will prevent you from saying the wrong thing." I continue to drag her down the street as she shivers and convulses in the throes of her second orgasm. The guards that are follow us seem to be highly amused by her plight and while it is not their place to think of themselves as above even my slave, I do tolerate there laughs if only for the sake of Macey's training. I smile to myself once again for I am now committed to making her into my slave.

After I watch her have what was probably only her second public orgasm, I surreptitiously cast the spell that will reveal how high her morality still is and am quite pleased, for while she was not yet low enough to be called even neutral her high moral standards and perceptions have fallen significantly, at least to the point where she can no longer regard herself as quite so morally superior to those around her. As we walk I take care not to go too fast for while it is easier on her knees it also allows more people to see and observe her and hopefully degrading her quicker. I continued to walk and chat with many and kept up a steady stream of 'zaps' on her so that by the time we arrive home she is in tears and crying through her gag, at the same time as squirming to find release from her lusts with anything she can reach.

Finally sitting in my favorite living room chain with her kneeling in the approved manner before me I pronounce, "Slave I don't enjoy killing you anymore and I'm sure you're not really thrilled with being butchered every day, am I right?" Seeing her nodding her head I continue, "Those morals

125

you prided yourself on for so many years are leaving you and with training you may even make a proper slave but you are not there yet. You see those three demons, they are my followers. My followers who will be rewarded by fucking you in each and every orifice, singularly or as a group and you will beg for more. They have my permission to use you in any and every way they can imagine and believe me a Succi Demon can be extremely imaginative in that particular direction. I will now remove the gag and you will then crawl over to them and beg to be used. You'll do that for your Mistress and you will do that now slave."

Sobbing as her mouth is freed and shuddering at the thought of what will soon be filling it, she looks up pleadingly but seeing the resolve on my face turns to crawl across the room and kneel with her knees far apart, offering herself. One of the guards laughs at her before standing, pulling out his cock from the amour on his groin and taking her hair in one hand guides her face to his rampant rod. He casually flicks his hips from side to side causing his cock to whip her face, slapping her cheeks as she sobs, the tears rolling down her cheeks, leaving tracks that are slashed by his cock, making his member damp.

"Perfect!" he goads, "Now you'll get to taste some salt on my meat open your mouth slave." As she opens wide he roughly tilts her face back before bending forward slightly and ramming his cock as far down her throat as he can, urged on by the jeers of his friends. The demon girl gags noticeably and tried to raise her hands to push him back but they are batted away by the others. He just snarls and presses the hard tip of his tail between her thighs, forcing it to enter her in a single painful thrust. She can not cry out but tries again to use her hands to push him away. At my nod the other two demons grab and chain her elbows together behind her, she can now only endure helplessly as his tail invades her and his cock chokes her.

The same two demons grab her by the hips and shoulders lifting her up so that her body is horizontal, belly down with the cock still deep in her throat and the tail punishing her pubis, letting her feet drop, one demon presses his cock into her ass from behind shoving hard enough to force the cock in her mouth even deeper down her throat. Her mews become moans as the cock is pulled from her mouth just in time to spurt creamy juices over her face. He drags his tail out still holding her by the hair and horns while the third demon uses her mouth for his turn. Leaning forward he slaps her ass hard enough to make the contact sound like a whip snapping. Two demons pump away under my watchful eyes as the first awaits his turn, to again install himself in whatever orifice he can get to.

I motion for Boyo to come to me, with quick apprehensive side glances at the foursome, he runs and kneels before me, eyes to the floor, "How may your slave serve you best Mistress?"

Looking down at him leaning forward to run my fingers through his hair and allay his fears, "The others who are on guard will need refreshments, take them demon meat and wine. And Boyo they are here to guard the household when their shifts are done tell them they can come and use the Inq captive to their pleasure. I need her morals removed as well as her spirit broken completely. I don't want you to become involved with the guards, you are mine and for my use only. Now, away with you then return here to please me."

His face radiates with relief as he leaves saying only, "Oh yes Mistress your slightest wish is this slaves desire."

Turning my attentions back to Macey I see that the arousing pheromones of three succi demons are working their magic and giving power to all four of them on the floor. Any pain she might have had, has been surrendered to passion and lust now as she rapaciously licks a cock before sucking it into her mouth. Her elbows are bound together still but rather than fight or even try to avoid the other demons she has joined in with enthusiasm and zeal. Actually the four are working together, two of them lift her by her hips and position her straddling the third demon lying on the floor, wearing only a smile and a huge erection, as they lower her onto his cock she arches her back maneuvering herself allowing the cock slides in effortlessly, her whole weight driving it deep inside herself. I hear her whimper then moan but as her arousal climbs she howls, begging for more.

I motion the guards away as I know now I have won the first battle. No Inquisitor will be able to summon her to London; she has been stripped of her morals now and can no longer even be thought of as an Inq, or more importantly can never be summoned to aid a mortal Inq again.

My next victory will come when she submits to me. Laughing to myself in anticipation I walk over to her then carefully hold the glass of wine for her to sip from. Smiling at her and giving her a kiss I let my forked tongue entwine her own. Her gaze rivets itself on me with the understanding that I will not have to kill her tomorrow, and I clearly hear the single word she stammers out, "Mistress?"

"Ah Mine your becoming such a sweet little lusty lady and you are having so much fun I'm very sure you will want to please the other three guards as they come off shift. The guards are due here any minute and they would prefer you clean and fresh so go now and use the shower but not for too long. I was watching you and I must say that you bring a whole new meaning to 'Four on the Floor,' my dear. She actually grins at my joke and I wave my hand to shoo her to the shower stall just off the room.

It is at that very moment I hear the clash of metal weapons in the outer rooms. Grabbing my trident I dash into the entrance room. There are nine of them all with their backs to the wall surrounded and cut off, one of my demon guards had magically spelled the door locked behind them so they have no place to retreat to. "Enough, you are far too late to do any good. Succi's take one step back but keep your weapons ready. The one you came for is no longer an Inq and has called me Mistress so leave now unharmed or be slaughtered where you stand."

The leader, a noble I had fought before snarls, 'Not even you can strip so much from her in such a short time. Prove what you say whore maker."

Calling her name loudly, I know I am gambling on her but have few options. "Macey come to your Mistress now girl!" She comes running naked glistening with the guards juices still covering her body and with the choke chain around her throat. I motion to the floor in front of me she immediately kneels with knees spread wide and breast high displaying her all to everyone. I am secretly ecstatic, but cannot blink yet. "Who is your Mistress Slave?"

Her rapid answer even as she sees her old cronies, brings a smile to my face. "You are Mistress."

I raised my eyes from her locking them on the leader before smiling and in my most imperious voice dismissing them, "You may go now." I nod to my followers, a word is spoken, a gesture is completed and the lock of the door thuds open. The nine of them shaking their heads in disbelief back from the room with weapons drawn, but leave they do.

They leave me with my guards, who all owe me fealty of sorts and now two slaves. Both of my slaves were taken from the house of Malthus. Both slaves captured, broken and enslaved by me. This revenge tastes so sweet that I simply have to share it with Mistress. Taking out the hell phone I do not even bother to return to my main living area before I use speed dial from the entrance we had almost fought over.

Chapter Thirteen

The hell-phone at Mistress's belt goes off again both startling her and alarming her, although the effect of seeing the device obviously impacts on Horatio. But after listening for several brief moments a smile spread across her face that matches a surge of pride mixed with increased security. Looking at Sugar she responds with satisfaction to the phone, "You have done well MINE, you make me proud to hold your leash." This news brings smiles to us all. We all, with the exception of Horatio, know of First Sister Spite's role in this and Mistress is signaling that the threat from hell has been dealt with. Horatio's look is of greater concern but he is still puzzled by the exchange. Mistress manages to have him relax slightly by saying, "Not to worry, merely one less barrier to the quest." These words seem to mollify him as he leads us to the room where his traveling supplies are kept.

The room is more like a combination office and bedroom complete with desk and chairs and a meticulously clean and spartan sleeping area. I peak around Mistress to stare inside as the room is too small for more than three or four people but I am shocked at the total lack of décor. Even my own slave pen now has an embroidered pillow and soft silky sheets, I have even tied individual strands of beads to hang down along the outer bars of the pen but this room is devoid of even the smallest of personal effects. This room is so scrupulously clean you can still smell a strong disinfectant. I just shake my head, for if this is how a High Inquisitor lives I am more than happy to be just a lowly Succi slave girl.

Needless to say he is quick and efficient less than ten minutes and he is fully packed and leading us through the warren of rooms that traverse the complex. In less time than I would have thought possible we are back to where we have left our weapons. But I feel it again in broad daylight, there peaking over the roof eave is a nightingale, without thinking I reach for my wand realizing too late it was still in the crate. Mistress looks at me, freezes for a single second, sees where I am looking and reaches down scoops up her dagger from the crate, leans back and throws the heavy weapon. The bird ducks back under the eave which now has a two foot long silver dagger embedded in it. Horatio wearing a baffled expression and every other Inq in the courtyard reaching for a weapon, Mistress without batting an eyelid, merely turns saying, "Sorry boys your appetizer just got away." Shaking the full length of her war whip out, she takes four strides backwards before bouncing forward three times and cracking her whip high above her head at the apex of her jump. The lash wraps itself around the hilt of the dagger dragging it out and down to where it is neatly caught by Mistress as she lands.

It may have been easy for the Inq's to dismiss Mistress's display of whip mastery, even if possibly at their peril but the glance that Mistress, Hex and I share speaks of our own private mysteries and concerns. Mistress's curt, "Everyone get your weapons! Doll on point with Dovey and Slice, we are going to the Catacombs next." This is as enough of a spur for us to form up rapidly and perhaps to even partly divert the attention of the Inq guards. As I bend to pick up my wand and charges Mistress whispered into my ear, "A tiny tease of these, oh so uptight gentlemen would not be out of order MINE."

As I stand up again I begin to do a stretch or two, pretending to limber up before continuing. Bending slightly forward making sure my breast armor is visible, I stretch out one leg while having my bottom jutting out behind and my shoulders thrown back and down. With nipple rings and chains now visible I slowly rotate my torso as every eye in the yard follows my gyration. Every eye except Sugar's who manages to pick the pocket of Horatio's man, Jansen. Seeing Mistress nod first to Sugar and then to me, I straighten, heft my pack and move forward with Slice and Dovey directly behind me. Two back from me I can hear Mistress and Horatio chatting while he questions Mistress as to why the three of us are leading rather than her.

"My Doll has eyes and ears that are superior to anyone's I have ever met, she sees, feels and hears better than the rest of us put together. If not for her, we would have all died already. Dovey has mapped all of the catacombs and her knowledge of them surpasses even how well you know the feel of your own sword in your hand. Her brother Slice is one of the most efficient killers I have ever met. I personally would lead but a good leader is able to recognize and utilize the strengths of others. I could lead us in and maybe even out, but they will see us all the way though." I am stroked by her thrill of pride knowing full well Mistress spoke in utter certainty but I resolve to concentrate on my job not on eavesdropping.

Dovey directs us to take the underground to Leister station and from there onto the aged and rusty rail tracks of the long abandoned Piccadilly Line. After walking less than five minutes she locates a crack in the wall and lighting a lantern indicates me to go through first, advising to be ready to fire fast. Thus prepared I slip through and dodge as a curved blade arcs close to my emerging head. Ducking and diving to roll into the cavern, I fire to the left as Slice comes through hacking to the right. Dovey just gives one body a kick before indicating a passage off to our left. This time the entrance to the cave is wide enough for three of us but also for the five beastlings that come charging out. I use my wand blasting straight ahead just as Dovey also fires her wand. But while my wand rips a fist sized hole in the ugly charging me, the wand Dovey uses hits three at the same time tearing and ripping through their flesh like a wave of steel. Before the first of these has fallen to the ground Slice has bisected the last from the top of its head to its crotch. We then proceed for a few minutes unopposed before once more the walls narrow; I hear the familiar sound of Robo-cops prowling. True to my ears there are three of them outside the doorway of what looks and sounds like a bar. Mistress Copper calls out to us all, "Check your supplies, we will spend the night here and this is the last chance to replenish before we go deeper so make sure you have enough water, charges and heals for the wands. Make sure you have a minimum of twenty full charges although thirty would probably be better."

Dovey takes me by the arm and leads me inside "I've seen you shoot, you're quite good but you will have more targets than you ever dreamed of so you had better stock up. Do you have more than twenty?" When I shake my head no, she waves a bar maid over saying, "I need about sixty full charges and a couple or maybe three hip flasks of dragon sweat to go sweetie."

As the girl moves off to get the order I notice just about everyone else is stocking up on this, that or the other thing. I even see Sugar put her hand to her throat and I overhear her whispering to Cyril how, "A good garrote has more than one purpose. You can strangle, trip, or whip with it and in a pinch I have even used one to keep a man from cumming before I wanted him to." I try not to snicker or even crack a smile but Cyril's face goes the pasty pale color of sun stained parchment.

Also close by Mistress is making arrangements for us to spend the night after we return while Slice seems ready to plunder as many of the barmaids' delights as he can grab even going so far as to assure at least three young lovelies he will be back for them tomorrow evening. Everyone seems to be in fine spirits except Horatio who is impatiently tapping his foot near the door. I just can't help but feel sorry for him and go over to the tall impressive man who must by his rank alone be a paragon of virtue. Not having met such people in the past I feel myself drawn to him. Smiling up I ask, "How long have you been with the Inquisitors, you seem very young to have such a high rank Sir?" He looks puzzled so I immediately try to put him more at ease, "This slave does not mean to bother you Sir or to be impertinent in any way but your traveling with us and sometimes knowing your friends is as important as knowing your enemies. Please don't take offense."

"Oh if that is your reason for approaching me, none taken but you must understand, I am Inquisitor and have very high moral standards. But to answer your question, Yes, I have advanced rapidly being under the temple tutelage rather than being taught by my predecessor, for only three years I have trained at the hand of the Demigod Thomas himself. But it was only when Malthus lost his best pupil and when he was censured by the temple that I was allowed to challenge his position. I defeated him with difficulty and he currently does penance in the temple. But what of you, you are very young to lead as experienced a party as this?"

I nod my head lowering my eyes encouraging him to think that I am not normally this brash but really remembering the man, that 'best pupil', I had so willing helped fuck and sacrifice with my sister Spite. "This poor slave is not a strong warrior but can often just feel an enemy or a threat, also her eyes, her wits and her ears are said to be very sharp, so traps seem easier to spot for me. This slave girl is still very young and has little experience knowing only two of the Succi spells but she grows in wisdom under Mistress's watchful eye." I look up at him, I feel my knees go weak; he is just too lovely to bear. My hands are itching to caress him and I am actually relieved when Dovey calls me away to get the extra charges she has ordered and a little surprised when she presses a hip flask into my pouch as well.

Giving me a conspiratorial wink, she quietly whispers, "It may very well be that our golden boy over there has a taste for spirits and unless I miss my guess, you will want to find this out some time later."

Smiling I accept the charges and flask from Dovey, at the same time I notice that Mistress is leaving the room, not being required to attend to anything in particular at the moment I follow Mistress as she goes to her room to help her with her armor. I can feel how tired Mistress is without even looking at her face so when she tells me to bring some hot water, towels and soap to clean her up, I hurry off returning as quickly as I can. Avoiding everyone else I arrive back before Mistress drifts off to sleep and admire her as she lays there naked. I carefully wash and dry her whole body finally using some of her oils to massage her tight shoulders until she closes her eyes surrendering to sleep at last. I feel so tired I just curl up beside her and drift off. I rise early even before Mistress wakes, carefully climbing from the bed so as not to wake her and hurry off to find some food to bring Mistress for her breakfast. I grab a bowl of grains that have been soaked overnight in yogurt and fruit for me, while I bring Mistress a meal of eggs, bacon, hash browns and orange juice. Mistress eats mostly in silence but finally says to me, "Doll you are as dear to me as any of MINE, you know that. But the Inq with us may represent a significant gain for my house. I know you shall obey me completely even when I tell you to do that which you do not understand but I want more love, so when I ask, if I ask, you shall act with all your heart understood?"

I do not understand what she means because I always try to obey but I can feel the sincerity in her. "Your slave will not fail you Mistress, your word is her command!"

Satisfied with my response she motioned to the trays, "I'll get myself ready love you just take this away and make sure the rest are getting dressed before you get yourself together, then come down to meet us all in the common room".

I do as I have been ordered quickly making sure everyone is up and has eaten. The last people to arrive in the common room are Dovey and Slice; she was delayed by having to drag Slice away from a shapely girl who had been serving him all night. She said she had to whack him over the head with the flat of his own sword before getting his attention. She comes over to me and slaps me on the behind saying, "Come girl your Mistress is outside already and as usual in a hurry, Slice you will have time enough for your adventures after Copper's so come along."

Outside after glancing at Mistress I go first, following Dovey's pointed finger, into the gloom of the many caverns connected in a maze that make up the catacombs. Our lanterns are lit and cast streams of light into the deep dark of the caverns. The first thing I notice is how they shine on the eyes of the beastlings that are massing near the end of the cave. Hearing swords unsheathed, I take out my wand and target just below one set of eyes and hear Mistress's Command, "On three, wands fire, One, Two, Three!" Beams of pure energy stab out into the darkness just as the mass of eyes begins to move rapidly toward us, many of that first wave of the beastling's charge, fall in that instant but far more are charging from behind. The front ranks are closer, I kept firing as fast as I possibly can, it seems that for every one that falls two more jump up in front of us but just as they are about to reach us the last of them dies. Not a single sword has drunk blood; it has all been wand work that has dissipated their ranks. But the carnage is something I have never experienced before. Bodies are deeply strewn like fallen leaves in the forest, all broken and useless now. I can't really say I am upset rather it is more like being numb. The uglies were going to kill us all so we defended. It is a nasty sight to see but rather them than me.

An Assassin's Quest

The wood of my wand is now warm, looking down I see that three of the charge containers are now just crumpled film, empty used completely in such a short time. I calculate thirty bursts of energy from my wand in less than three minutes and wonder if I should have got more charges. I know from experience that it will mean at least nine trips to the 'Altar' to recover enough sperm to make that many magical charges.

Fortunately after that attack there are only occasional encounters with the uglies and never in any great numbers. But the killing goes on so that by the time we stop for our first break and some water yet another charge is gone.

Shortly we forge ahead once more spending the remainder of the morning traveling in the murky maze. Now all around us we see minerals in the walls and strange lichens that glow briefly when crushed. As we pass through the many passages and rooms of the catacombs I can readily see that there are streaks of white milky rock veins that hold threads of silver or at times even golden ore in them. But still later we arrive at an area littered with tiny stones that range in size from minuscule to pea, with some almost like small gravel and very rarely the occasional fist size rock.

This is where Mistress calls again for a stop for lunch. While I eat a carrot and some dried meat I pick up and inspect one small rock. I am startled, I realize that this is in fact an uncut diamond; automatically I tuck it away for Mistress. When we start off again both Dovey and Slice seem to be particularly nervous. Just as we turn a corner into a large chamber taking only about ten steps, I catch the now familiar whiff of an ugly. Raising my hand even though I cannot see any assailants, Dovey barks, "Yes my dear I had expected a large attack to have occurred already, so get ready but this time we must keep moving through them as they attack." It is at this very moment at the outer edge of the range of our lanterns that all of the eyes open at the same time, hundreds of them; I fire shooting to kill. Dovey's

137

wand needs to be closer so she runs ahead with both Slice and Horatio followed closely by Cum while I blast away at the uglies, carefully shooting between them. Dovey is ahead to my left with Slice beside her, Mistress is to my right with Crap hacking away by her flank. The crack of Mistress's whip mingles with the hiss of wands and the solid thuds of swords slashing into flesh and bone. A fireball blooms in front of us and into that gap, side by side step Horatio and Slice each bellowing their individual war cries. The rest of us come behind blasting, hacking and lashing our way through the crowded cavern sometimes almost tripping over piles of fallen bodies but always relentlessly moving ahead.

My wand is now quite hot from constant use but as suddenly as the assault had begun it tapers off and ends. Looking behind us I see the many bodies scattered like broken crockery on a kitchen floor. We have advanced about half way through the long narrow cavern to the point where there is a smaller entrance leading off to one side, when something catches my eye. There it is again, I see something glint in the beam of the lantern light and I dart ahead between Slice and Horatio. Kneeling, I hold up a hand to stop everyone as I see four fine wires stretched tightly across the center of the cavern. Holding the lantern high I peer off to the sides trying to find where they come from. The wires are connected to both of the walls on either side of us. They all look in shock as I point to the walls noticing that these walls are different from the ones we have been passing, these consist of piles of stones behind vines strung like webbing. Both to our left and right huge rocks and stones are held back by the mesh that extends all the way to the ceiling. This is a dead fall trap and looking at the mass of rock on the walls, we would certainly have been dead if they had fallen on us, for it covers most of the cavern we had been fighting in. If anyone had hit or even touched the wires we would all be dead. I call for Cyril and Sugar to help as they have very nimble fingers and know traps far better than I know my name.

As Cyril sees what I have found he turns white and staggers saying, "I believe that someone really does not want to be disturbed. This has not been here for too long perhaps a week or at the most a month." He points to some discarded scraps of food on the other side of the wires. But Sugar whispering as she confers with him finally nods and motions everyone else back beyond the place where the rocks would fall. I hold the lantern high to give them more light and watch them start by hammering spikes into the floor. They space the spikes in a row running back toward the walls. Secondly very carefully each of them holds one side of the first wire before cutting it between them. I can see them strain to keep the tension exactly steady as individually they move back and attached each of the wires to a spike. They have to repeat this three more times; it seems to me that every time they cut another wire our tension increases, I know that I am shaking by the time they tie off the last wire to a spike.

With that last wire secure we all heave a sigh of relief and move forward into the cavern once again. Looking to either side I shiver as I truly appreciate that those tons of rock would have turned this into a gallery of death for us. I also realize now that not all traps are passive, the only way we would not have noticed the webbing on the walls is if we were fighting. Someone has gone to a great deal of trouble on this trap, a someone I really do not want to meet. But I move on leading where Dovey directs me, until finally we arrive at a set of metal doors some five feet high. Dovey whispers in my ear, "I have only been this far three times before but have never been through the door, yet I know this area well and it is more than possible that there are four other passageways leading to what is beyond the door." Not touching it I motion to Cyril and Sugar to come and help me check for traps but no one can detect any trace of deception or devise, the doors merely swing inward as no lock is even apparent. Moving even closer I peer through the central crack of the door and see a lit room with a great many figures moving about. Turning, pressing my finger to my lips, I go back to

Mistress and whisper my report of what I have just seen. She looks at our party shrugs in resignation and in a whisper tells us to form up for a charge through the doorway.

Checking my charges I realize I have been through over twenty for when we left the bar I had fifty full charges with me. Now I have fewer than thirty left so resolve to make every shot count. Hex sucks back a potion of power and began to cast boosts on us all. Dovey slaps her belt buckle and the deadly diamond edged tutu sprouts up, Cyril is grasping a pair of daggers almost shaking, while both Horatio and Slice take out their blades and kiss them as only a lover could. This time Mistress steps to the front war whip in her right hand and silver dagger in her left and after taking two steps back, jumps forward to kick the door open charging in screaming a single raw, scathing, primordial note.

There must have been at least fifty heavily armed and armored uglies that turn towards Mistress's war cry. Of those ten are dead before they even see her. The rest charge but are killed within seconds but the other doors opens and more enemies pour in from four directions. I fire as fast as I can; isolating each target in turn for every single one of my shots needs to kill.

"We have to keep them out! Push them back through the doorways and hold them there!" Mistress shouts out to us even as we attack. Using my wand now from the hip, I can feel the wood begin to rapidly heat but I keep on firing until we push them back out of the doors. With Horatio and Mistress in front of me I glance around and see that everyone is taking a stand at a door except Cyril, who is neither on guard nor fighting instead he has gone to a large chest in the exact center of the room and has begun work on the lock of the chest but I spare not a single thought for Cyril as I scan the room, for at that very instant I sense another of those damn birds. I feel and fire catching it in mid-flight. Looking back I see that with Mistress's whip and Horatio's sword guarding the doorway I am totally superfluous so I move back to join Hex in the center of the room and hear the cry from behind me. Turning I see Cyril impaled with a spike that has shot up from the floor beneath him. The spike has gone through his stomach creating a wound that in moments will be fatal. The spike has gone right through his stomach and out his back. There is horror, fear and shock being written across his face as he straightens pulling himself free from the horrible pain of the spike. In an almost reflexive action I focus all my thoughts, my whole mind on the first page of my spell book; I see the spell in my mind's eye while rushing towards him. The geysers of blood spurt from wounds that are so big I can almost see inside him, I know he is dying ; I let the spell go. It slips from me like a cooling evening breeze that wraps around and through him. What has been broken, every tiny bit of him that was whole before being rent and torn apart is rapidly rejoined. I feel all those wounds reunite as the energy for the change is sucked out of me. The gore in his stomach, where blood had flowed freely rapidly closes as his wound heals from the inside out. I help to pull him upright supporting his weight as I drag him back as yet another spike suddenly juts up from the floor.

"I got it all," he moans still in shock and pain. "I never noticed that last trap trigger until it was too late but I have all we came for."

I see three more spikes quickly pop up from the floor this time further out from the chest. I shout out urgently, "Mistress it is done, we have what we came for. This room is trapped Mistress please we have to leave now!" Still supporting Cyril who carries a heavy leather sack with him, I move toward the entrance we had originally entered through. I hear Mistress's voice boom out to everyone, "You heard her! Fall back to the entrance fast but let's make this orderly. We are not scavenging rabble but the best they have ever seen so make them pay with every step back we take."

Cyril is starting to take more of his own weight now that the pain of his near fatal wound is wearing off. As I step through the doorway I can still feel him shaking but he seems a bit stronger. Just as I pass, we are grabbed from either side of the door. I barely have time to shout a warning before a hand covers my mouth. Biting down into the flesh of that hand I almost gag at the vile taste, I kick down hard on a foot as I can try to twist free. The hand leaves my mouth but fastens on my other arm. Held helpless to resist and seeing more coming I can think of only one option for me. I remember the spell I had used by mistake; it comes to my mind like a lover to a bed.

I steal the moment as I visualize the spell of seduction; I smile and moan then jut my breasts forward and see a look of awe overcome the features of the ugly. He frees me instantly and kneels before me; he even starts to remove his armor. Not that he has much of a chance as I reach down grabbing his hair right before taking out a dagger and slashing through his throat. Spinning I see Cyril struggling with his own captor just as Mistress's whip and Slice's sword tear the assailant apart. The rest of the party comes through the door rapidly with Dovey blasting between Crap and Horatio who are slashing and hacking at a hoard that follows close behind.

We all move backward one step at a time fighting a running battle through the cavern, until we come to the place where the wires had been tied to spikes. Mistress say, "Fireballs all. Smoke 'em if you have 'em, then run like mad!" I understand what she needs and just before we pass the point where the beastlings feet will trip the trap I send out witheringly rapid fire from my wand totally exhausting my supply of charges and run for my life. The explosion is immense perhaps seven fireballs going off at the same time along with my own fire. That deafening blast combined with the heat is horrific; the true terror as we run is that the walls behind us to either side start to collapse like dominos covering the army behind us. It is tight, very tight for as Dovey the last of our party burst through the passage entrance, the ceiling of the chamber behind us collapses on the pursuing army blocking the route behind us completely.

Coughing in the blinding dust blowing out of the cavern I realize my wand is so hot the wood is starting to smoke. But when Mistress calls for us to say our names, everyone who had left the bar answers in their turn. Shaking ourselves off and wiping the grime from our faces we all gratefully drink some water. I remember the flask Dovey had given me and take a short pull of fortifying spirits. Horatio is standing beside me coughing, I do what I would have liked someone to do for me and pass him the flask. He responds with a shy smile but takes the flask and sips, rinsing out his mouth before spiting it out on the ground. He follows up his sip with a man sized pull before handing it back to me.

"Not only can you find traps young lady, but you also know when to pass the ammo." He says with a laugh, "Your Mistress chose well when she put you on point."

Taking the flask back I just smile and look down not wanting to lose whatever respect I had earned from him. Hearing Mistress call me back to the lead, I dutifully step once more in front.

We move quickly even though some of us need to be helped particularly Hex who is so exhausted she is barely coherent. But stumbling sometimes, running other times, gasping we make our way through the catacombs with Dovey and I leading until we reach the final turn and see the Robocops patrolling outside the bar.

Looking around at our party, we are dust covered, clothes and armor rent and torn. Cum walking tall, holding Hex in his arms looking around him ready to challenge any comers, his manner and expression stoic but proud. Crap walking with a limp her dust stained cheeks streaked by tears of exhaustion; even Dovey's bright colors have been muted by blood, dust and sweat, the expression on her face is drained, strained and tired, but still proud and without remorse. I do not need to see Mistress to know she has been shocked by how strong the opposition was today. But in the midst of shock there is now a burning pride of those around her that is threatening to bring tears to her eyes. Slice walks with his head held high with one hand holding his sword rested on his shoulder while the other partly supports an exhausted Taken. Sugar walks close by Cyril both of them appear to be dazed and exhausted by the events of the day although they seem somehow closer than they were before. For my own part I probably look a sight, covered in dust, sweat, grime and not a little blood, although none of the latter was mine. I had left carrying a wand that had been made of a light colored wood so blonde it was almost the same shade as my hair; now that same wand is a rich ebony color. The pack that held fully fifty charges is empty; I suck in my cheeks realizing it will take over 150 trips to the Altar to replace all those charges.

Strangely one person is different, seemingly almost reveling in the day. He is the one who now walks in Slices place behind me and he, Horatio is unique in that he seems somehow to still be pristinely clean. His stride is still long and true; it almost looks as if he has just returned from some light exercise. He looks so good he almost glows.

Mistress turns to me while her and I are very close to Horatio, "Doll love I know you are tired but an Inquisitor General normally has an aide to assist him after a battle, tonight you will be that aide. Make sure his clothes and armor are cleaned and repaired. Take care of his weapons as well as assist him in any and every manner possible is that clear MINE?"

Horatio protests, "No wait that girl has done a hero's duty more times than enough today, it was her that carried the day she needs her rest as much or more than anyone here."

I wanted to kill him then but Mistress knows that. "Damn you Horatio, do you think me some sort of barbarian that I can not or will not provide you with the comforts and services you are accustom to? You fought well today and normally this would be your due. For you to refuse this would be the same like slapping me in the face. So just take advantage of it rather than insulting me and MINE." Then looking closer at me she sort of snorts, "Although I do admit she could probably do with a little clean up herself."

I turn to him with my eyes lowered and dip one knee saying, "Please Sir, do not shame this slave in front of her Mistress."

He just shakes his head in resignation, "If you're going to be my aide then you better come with me now but none of that Succi nonsense, I'm an Inquisitor General and do have certain standards to maintain." After saying that he just huffs once turns saying, "Come along then girl."

After he turns Mistress smiles almost giggles and winks at me. I know then exactly what is expected of me and just how much I want it.

Chapter Fourteen

I thought of the demon that used to be called Macey. She had attacked my favorite sister, destroyed her voice, and I had harried the harlot hater through hell. That was what Mistress had commanded but I had gone much further than that. I had turned her holy hypocrite perspectives against her. I had broken her for now she is MINE. She has not yet begged to become MINE; I have not yet given her the chance but rather I just took her instead.

But now today I will reward her after I find the perfect collar for her formerly blue throat. I have to admit the selection before me in terms of both quality and diversity is only exceeded by the attentions of the syrupy sales sleaze that is attempting to attend to my requests. He is atrocious, he has brought out a beautiful piece, a high necked silver collar studded with green gems but his greasy fingers mar the surface. I just put my fingers to my temples and inhale deeply. I do not lose my temper, rip his eyes out or even give him the verbal lashing he so richly deserves. I merely look at him coldly, "I think perhaps I would like to speak with your owner." In a deliberate attempt to emphasis my displeasure my words now drop like ice nuggets from my lips, "Tell him that I would be better served by someone who actually gives a damn." Turning from the hapless clerk I decide to wait for his owner after all the selection is quite good even if the server needs a whipping.

The owner a demoness, who moves with grace and style, addresses me directly. "Is there a problem Baroness?"

Pointing a talon at the finger prints on the collar recently shown, I merely ask, "And would you have me place that spoiled piece on the throat of an obedient and valued slave?"

Seeing the tarnished silver she turns and glares, "You dog, home with you now! And prepare my whips for when I return." She nods her head in appreciation to me. "That one has a significant amount of learning to do for while he tries hard he seems most adept at failure. But let me show you something perhaps a bit more to your liking, something untarnished and pristine." She bends to the bottom of a display case casting a minor unlocking spell that pops open a hidden drawer, from this she takes out a unique piece, partially wrapped in velvet it is an exquisitely jeweled gold and white gold collar. It is merely an inch and a half wide but its lower edge narrows in two spots enabling it to more easily rest on the widening of the neck over the shoulders. It is also lined with soft black leather but most astounding is the way the gold has been cut through along the upper and lower edges, forming two intricate borders of small diamond shaped openings each outlined with white gold and separated from each other only by a tiny jewel also set in white gold.

I gasp this is a truly astounding piece, it even has a number of empty mountings for gems to be embedded in, gems no doubt that would be chosen to highlight the beauty of the wearer's skin, eyes or hair. Looking at it closely I can see it is a collar that will have to be sized and fitted to the wearer before being riveted into place. This is a permanent collar, one that will only come off with the head. I look up and smile, "This is for MINE I shall bring her here for her fitting so DO NOT sell it; I want you to engrave the name 'Spite's Slut' on it then place bright green emeralds in those empty fittings. I shall return for it later, you may collect your payment at your discretion take my ring to the Bank of Satan, present it there in exchange for your due and leave the ring with them." With that I leave the ring on the counter, not counting or caring the cost, for this piece must be on MINE.

I hurry home a smile on my face but enter looking sternly about. I had not retained all the guards who had developed a fondness for over using my girl but kept three on knowing that Mistress is able to get a war going at the drop of a proverbial tear. I call both Boyo and Macey to me, and have them kneel in front of me for inspection. "Strip now! Both of you, and do it quickly." Taking out my riding crop, I bring it to first Boyo's then Macey's lips to kiss before taking hold of Macey's choke chain and snapping a leash on Boyo's Collar. "On all fours," I hiss, "you are both going to be my pets in the market today."

Taking both their leads, I slowly stroll with them behind me out of the house and down the street to the market area; thinking not only of the truly lovely collar I had commissioned but also of the howls that sales slave deserves to be screaming. Both of my naked slaves are unused to this treatment although both have experienced it before but they had better become accustom to it in a hurry, as I do so enjoy having my pet's on the ground behind me. I have my riding crop in hand just in case one of them should so much as blink wrong.

If I'm going to take the trouble to walk them they had better behave especially where we are going. When we arrive I am greeted by the smiling face of the proprietor as she indicates where the fitting room is. Dropping Boyo's leash I see him automatically go to the kneeling position with his eyes suitably lowered a gentle smile on his face as I ruffle his hair with the very tips of my talons. I lead Macey into the fitting room, "Kneel MINE and listen carefully. You are my slave I took your freedom in honorable combat and later accepted your complete surrender. Now it is time others know exactly that. Your name has been Macey and as I took your freedom, I took your name as well. Henceforth you shall be called 'Spites Slut' and will wear that name as long as your head remains on your shoulders. Do you understand girl?"

She looks up at me with the beginnings of tears in her eyes, but in voice heavy and hoarse, replies, "Yes Mistress!"

Taking her choke chain off her neck easily and guiding her to a workbench where the proprietor stands watching. Holding out my hand for the Collar I carefully inspect it, feeling each of the seven embedded gems for lose ness and examining the etching in detail. Satisfied I hold it out for her to see. Here my dear is a thing of great beauty. Gold co-joined with white gold and gemstones are all fashioned with skill in to the most beautiful of collars. This is what you shall wear for all eternity as my slave. Now tell me your name.

There is a look of awe in her eyes when she sees the collar, it is an exquisite piece of art and she knows it. But she shivers when she replies quietly, "Spite's Slut." I frown fingering my riding crop and she looks up in panic saying louder, "Spites Slut Mistress your eager slave."

Smiling gently I lead her forward and bend her head over a small anvil on a low work bench. There the proprietor eases the collar around her throat fitting it tightly before using chalk to mark nine spots on either side of the metal. The collar is removed again and carried to another part of the bench where each one of the nine marks is drilled. While this is happening I stroke her hair cooing softly to her of how beautiful she will be with that collar. I can see that she is uneasy but starting to relax just a bit. So I ask, "Could you ask for anything sweeter my slut? Isn't this exactly what you have always wanted?"

She looks up at me eye's wide, but now much more composed, "This slave can never again say no to you Mistress, what happened has made her who she should have been all along."

I kiss her brow then as the demonic jeweler returns with the treasure for my treasure. I feel so good while I press her head to the anvil and see the nine rivets fastening my slave into her collar forever.

I look up as the jeweler leaves with a nod. Taking my new slave by the horns pulling her to me with a grin I force her head between my thighs. I can feel no resistance from her but rather I hear her inhale my scent deeply and deliberately her fingers fly to the fastenings of my armored thong releasing it quickly and easily. Her mouth opens and her forked tongue darts in and out licking, lapping like tiny twin forks of lightening. Sighing I lift my thigh over her shoulder telling her what a good girl she is before biting my lips in sheer pleasure. Her tongue, her lips are making me throb. I feel lust and love and life pulse like a well fueled fire in my loins. I moan without reservation just before a shattering orgasm, clenching my thighs so tight I know she has no way to breathe. I feel her tongue weaken and stop before I free her to gasp for air once again. Her body driven once more by my pheromones shudders as she climaxes herself then she places her forehead on my foot in thankfulness and to show her adoration.

Chapter Fifteen

I meekly follow Horatio inside and all the way to the end of the hall where his room is located. His stride is longer than mine, even longer than I remember while he was with the party; it is almost as if he is running away from me. When I had been here before I took careful note of which rooms are being used by whom, as well as remembering where the baths and laundry are located. While I must admit that the smells coming from the kitchen are almost as enticing as the strong male body striding in front of me; I also have to wonder if that body might well be lured with food as well.

I have had a very rigorous day that has taken a lot out of me but being close to him seems to give me back that little bit needed to continue. I just drop my dusty pack in the corner and excuse myself saying, "I'll be right back for your clothes Sir. If you have them ready, I'll get them cleaned for you." Slipping into the laundry I strip naked removing the parts of my clothing that can be washed and also leaving my precious armor that now shows tears in the mail and dents in the plate for repair. My going back to the room naked except for my rings, chains and collar is not an accident but rather an overt enticement. I find him dressed in a long white robe with his armor and clothes neatly folded to one side. Not wanting my intentions to be seen as quite as blatant as they really are, I gather his things up trying not to look at him directly and scurry out to have the clothes washed and the armor attended to. Going back towards the room I hear his voice coming from the baths, I can't help but smile at the thought of him naked. I abruptly change direction to the tubs.

Slice, Cum and Cyril have joined him already and I know that the others will soon be on their way to try out the double pools of steamy bubbly water. I slide into the tub from behind him while he is looking in the other direction, slipping up closely to him so that my legs will have to occasionally brush against his. I announce my presence by letting him know what I have done, "Your armor is being repaired and polished Sir, the slaves here have much more skill with that than this poor slave and your clothes are being laundered as well. The attendants have been instructed to bring your clothes and armor back to your room when they are ready. Your sword and knives, this girl will hone after she is clean enough to touch them Sir." I say all this very softly in a low throaty voice so that he has to lean closer to me to hear me over the bubbling waters.

His response is louder than it needed to be, almost as if he is making up for my soft whisperings. "Thank you Copper's Doll but you do not need to sharpen my blades only I take care of those."

"Oh no Sir, Mistress would punish this poor slave if she were not to serve you in this manner." I plead earnestly, "Please don't make Mistress punish this slave again two days in a row would be too much to endure." It is a gamble but then I stand up in front of him and turn my back, first showing him myself naked but then displaying the still red scars and welts from the whipping that I had endured yesterday morning. His cough is enough to assure me that I will not be excluded from his room tonight, standing with my back to him I just wink at Cum, Slice and Cyril. The tub we are in should really have held only one more but both Sugar and Taken slide in to join us. Soon I am squeezing in much closer to Horatio, everything must have seemed reasonable to him for he does not complain but only tries in vain to keep a little distance although I am not going to let that happen. I am sure Mistress told both of my sisters to get in the tub for exactly that reason.

I smile when Mistress comes over to the edge of the tub and congratulates Cyril on retrieving the Chalice and Skulls. His response is a little strained, "That damn spike trap was on the last skull in the chest and for some reason there was only eleven skulls not twelve. But if you look in the pocket of my tunic there was something else I just grabbed. It is a tiny scroll but who knows it may have some value to those who can read it."

Mistress nods in satisfaction after retrieving the scroll and hands it to Hex before speaking to all of us at once, "It has been a very long hard day and I have asked the owners here to serve us supper along the edge of the tubs. We still have a lot to do to complete this quest but after this arduous day I think it may be wise to rest a little rather than press on. If today showed anything it is that there seems to be more at play than any of us know. There is not even a mention in history about that many beastlings fighting together, much less setting traps as deadly as we saw today. Before dawn the day after tomorrow, I want every one of you in top form, fully armed and ready to fight again. So enjoy yourselves tonight as we still have to figure out where the third item, the brass bell is hidden." Taking their cue from Mistress, Sugar makes more room in the tub by sitting on Cyril's lap in the most accommodating way as Taken moves to kiss Slice's neck.

Looking up excitedly from the far side Hex almost shouts, "I think not Mistress. This is a very old document it lists several items that are and I quote, 'stored in hiding,' there is a brass bell mentioned as being under a flagstone in the National Maritime Museum along with other items I really do not understand. That place is actually very close to our home."

Mistress seems pleased but I can still feel she is worried that this silver lining has some serious tarnish to it somewhere. "I know that the wand users went through an extreme amount of charges today. It would be highly appropriate for those to be replaced. But at least Doll has not had to waste any shots on those stupid birds."

Sadly I shake my head saying, "No Mistress in the room of five doors your slave felt and saw one that was about to attack Master Cyril, that one died particularly fast." I can almost hear the grinding of tooth against tooth as Mistress turns her gaze on me.

All she says is, "If you are truly sure it is dead there can be no fault on you sweetling but you must be very sure or we have to dress, rearm and sally forth tonight to kill the thing."

Shocked and stunned that Mistress would even consider such a thing, I put all the certainty I can muster into my response. I am certain that it is dead and Mistress now knows that even before I speak. "The shot was at close range Mistress no more than ten feet, I saw it hit, I saw it burn, I even smelled the burning feathers. It is dead!"

Horatio looking confused asks, "And this is important why?"

It is Hex, standing there completely nude and completely hairless who answers the query, "If we knew Sir we could tell you, but these birds, Nightingales, have been spying on us. They are good at hiding in the gloom of night or caves. Only Doll can really kill them since they seem to notice anyone else trying to target them and fly away. They also carry in their little heads tiny golden components of science or magic, those are totally alien to anything known in London."

Horatio looks at me again but this time in a different manner as if he is now seeing someone that is not just the slave of those who are not his compatriots. He looks intrigued by me almost as if I am a person that is

An Assassin's Quest

much more interesting and mysterious. I have to look away. I just shrug, "This girl has sharp eyes and gets an itch up her spine whenever those awful birds spy on us there is nothing special in that." But do I notice that I am now allowed to cuddle a little closer underneath the water.

Fortunately the food arrives so I am able to divert attention away from me. I grab a rib and a stein of beer and bring it to Horatio. Patiently I hold his beer for him as he devours the meat. As he finishes the rib I gently lift the bone from his fingertips replacing it with the stein grabbing another rib in the process. This time rather than offer it to him I hold it for him to eat from my hand murmuring, "Please let this slave serve you Sir."

He glances first to Mistress before he just looks at me with a quizzical smile, "Doll you have been instructed to aid me and I would entertain no breach of propriety here."

Mistress turns to us, she is just ready to enter the other tub and is totally naked but rather than continue to set foot in the water she walks over to the two of us, "Horatio I want you to look at the scars on my body, each and every one of them have been honorably earned in combat and mostly against Inqs sent by your predecessor. I have had 16 years of fighting but you; with Doll in your arms represent perhaps our last, best chance of ending this crap. Make no mistake, Doll is MINE, by my collar and my brand and in other way's you could not understand. But while you're with us, to maybe help end this war you are welcome to her."

He looks up at Mistress scrutinizing her even though her nudity obviously makes him uneasy. Glancing down briefly before he answers, "Thinking on Thomas's confusing behavior I really am not sure that either of us have a whole lot of choice here. But always keep in mind that first, last and always I am who I am, the Inquisitor General and that may cut short a great deal of options for you and me later. Yet this here and now is a different sort of affair, we both know something was very wrong with what happened today. It could be as I recently heard Thomas say, 'What was must pass and what will be must come and that change will make us stronger or crush us utterly.' So perhaps at long last it is time for all of us to stand side by each and back to back as we all did so well today."

He looks around first at Taken who, as if on cue has just settled her delightful ass on Slice's cock then over to Sugar and Cyril who are beginning to make waves of their own and finally to Dovey and Cum energetically bumping and grinding away. Visibly embarrassed at first, he then merely shakes his head in confusion, looks heavenward and sighs.

I don't really understand what he has said but I'm so happy at what Mistress has just said that I turn to him beaming, unconsciously licking my lips in anticipation. Glancing back up at Mistress before turning to me, he sets the beer stein down, takes the rib bone from my fingers and tosses it over his shoulder saying, "Ah such sweet duty. Who am I but to answer its clarion call?" His arm slips under the water with his hand behind me he pulls me in closer kissing me deeply.

Almost as one breaking a fast he hungrily does not terminate that kiss for many minutes but when he does, I lean back breathlessly slightly repositioning myself, with one leg is over his hips. I smile at Mistress, "Your Slave thanks you for the opportunity to serve Mistress." As I lower my lips to his throat I place one hand over his shoulders and lower the other under water where I find his rapidly hardening cock. Sounds seem to blur around me, bubbling water, voices chatting, the sound of all merging and falling back out of my perception. All day long my senses have been on full alert scanning, searching, and seeking out danger, now all that slips away as I let my awareness submerge into sensation. Hungry for release I taste the salty skin of his throat with my lips; I can feel the pulse in his throat quicken as I stroke his cock beneath the water. Looking up, looking directly into his eyes

I slide my splayed hips up so I can thrust down on to his cock and begin to gently roll my bottom while riding his steel shaft. There is no need for a Zap, not for him nor for me but rather his pent up lust drives us on. With the roll of my hips, the squeeze of my thighs engulfing his cock I begin to rock back and forth, lifting myself then sliding down his length.

As if Mistress had ordered we are far from alone in our activities, for although several others have moved into the other pool it seems as if everyone is feeling more alive and enthusiastically celebrating the survival of our second day of the quest, seeming to have a greater lust for life having come so close to death. In our frenzy we are all whipping the water into surging surf. Now that we have more room Horatio stands, turning me with my back to the pool side, resting my shoulders on the edge allowing me to brace myself and respond to his deep thrusting hips. Arching my back as I feel him fill me he hammers on driving me further out of the water. Mistress is with both Crap and Hex in the other tub and her arousal is so linked to mine that there are five simultaneous eruptions of passion, my own cries mingling with those of Mistress echo in my head. Finally he exhausts himself and pulls me close to kiss and cuddle. I murmur in his ear telling him how good and how strong he is but I don't lie as he really does feel so good, maybe even better because he truly seems to in believe me. This time when I raise a rib bone to his lips to eat, he pulls my head close so we can gnaw on the same bone together and enjoy the taste of the succulent meat in the rich red sauce. In comparing it to Pepper's I realize just how great a cook she really is because even with the company I am keeping this pales in comparison.

But seeing a number of the other girls head off I remember my duties and beg to leave, not telling Horatio that I am going to seek out an 'Altar' as well as a water closet. I climb onto the 'Altar' and snuggle into it, relaxing as my body is invaded by the three hoses of the 'Altar'. Feeling the squirting and suctioning actions of the hoses that throb inside me is the start of yet another lovely little orgasm and a pleasant prelude to the removal Horatio's sperm. The sperm that later will be turned into potions of power to fuel our magic or to create the charges for my wand. For every potion to cast ten spells takes two trips to the 'Altar' and every charge holding ten shots for my wand takes three. Upon leaving the 'Succi Altar' room I see both Cyril and Sugar leave with the manager, I look quizzically at Sugar but can see no sign of concern or distress. So I merely go about my business glad that I have had the chance to climb again on the 'Altar' and start the process of replenishing the vast amounts of stored magical energy I had used.

If had eavesdropped I would have discovered what Sugar was up too. For she and the manager took Cyril to a hidden room. There Cyril was introduced to the Chief Assassin who is the head of the Assassin's Guild in the Catacombs. Sugar has been teaching Cyril her trade in the hopes of properly recruiting an assassin assistant. She had long ago mastered both the weapons and the stealth of her trade and it is her duty to pass on her knowledge and being in the one place where a master assassin who specializes in poisons of every type was just too good to pass up. Later Cyril would owe a certain amount of fealty to the man for the knowledge he receives but he would be under the direct command of Sugar as long as he walks the 'Path of the Grave Fillers'.

Sugar's whole world has been Mistress Copper for many years but before Mistress, she too had been trained as an assassin. At the time only Spite had known and it was the last thing she had held back before she had given herself to Mistress Copper. Since those bygone days much had happened and she had risen to become the Chief Assassin in not only one but two districts of London; it was for this reason she knows the true identity of the 'Lost Assassin', the one who rules them all. It is her responsibility to recruit and train newcomers as well as to make sure the commissions they take do not infringe on existing alliances and are carried out in a timely manner.

Cyril was showing promise, even though he really had more courage than he gave himself credit for and his nimble fingers were easy for her to train. Although so tired she was literally lightheaded, still she continued with his training. She grimaces knowing that he may not ever be the best assassin around but he would be the best she could make him which meant that while he would never wear her collar, his loyalty to her would be well established.

Chapter Sixteen

When I return to the tub room I find that Horatio has left already but Mistress is still there. As I kneel in front of her she nods to me, "Mine you have done well. You started yesterday under my lash but have since caused me to walk with pride for two whole days. But don't lose it now, he may be an Inquisitor General but he is young, proud and strong and will make a far better ally than enemy. That is your job, to have him acknowledge that I own you but also to have him still desire to be with you badly enough to want to work with us. So go to my pack, take out the silks and oils and go ease his aching muscles. I want you to become a VERY good friend to him."

I beam and readily answer, "Oh yes Mistress, with the greatest of pleasure Mistress." She only chuckles and motions me to go then embraces Hex and Crap in her happiness. When I reach his room and enter quietly I find him fast asleep. I slide in behind gently spooning him with my arms over his back, holding him close in my embrace.

Much later I wake up to a warm but empty bed. Stretching before I arise helps me to get out of bed without wincing, yesterday had been a very long one and the tension I had held in my back, neck and shoulders is making itself known by causing unpleasant tightness today. Thinking back I realize just how momentous the quest has been so far. My role in finding traps and guiding the party has now been established, being punished for casting my first spell, meeting not one but two Demigods, receiving my first spells and using them both in a horrendous battle, all of these have let us fulfill just two parts of the quest. Moreover I have a lover now and not just because of Mistress's command and he is just not going to get away!

I grab a couple of towels one to drape over my shoulders, the other I tie around my waist, I really am not worried about appearing naked in the bar but knowing Horatio's past, a certain level of modesty might arouse him more by having only glimpses of what he enjoyed last night. The majority of the party is in the room with the twin tubs all relaxing or chatting, although noticeably absent are Sugar, Cyril, Mistress and Crap and mores the pity, so is Horatio. Dovey and Slice are chatting with Cum and Taken and when I come in we share both coffees and wraps filled with egg, bacon and onions. There are a few other patrons still slurping on beers or nibbling on taste treats while just lounging in the pool and being served and serviced by some of the many girls here. It is still early in the day but one of the patrons obviously must have started drinking very early or had not stopped his carousing from the night before. When Dovey gets out of the tub and leaves to relieve herself, I notice him snort into his cup rolling his eyes at another patron but his attention is soon diverted by a server he clearly desires for he gets out of the tub and goes over to her, trying to pull her close for a kiss. The girl is as nimble as he is drunk and easily evades him, leaving to get refills and ignoring his calls for her. It is then that Dovey re-entered moving past him on her way to the tub. "Hey you, yeah you, the short fat one, why don't you get out of here? You're spoiling everybody's view of the nice looking girls." Suddenly a silence descends on the room; everyone is almost holding their breath in horror of what Dovey will do. Her response seems very slow in coming almost as if she is unsure of herself as she walks over to him. When he sees her coming he pretends to stick his finger down his throat and retch but then gloats, "Damn even the fat ones want it."

Dovey's head is only a bit higher than his waist but she looks up smiles then faster than a snake she reaches out grabs his ball tightly sneering quite loudly, "I'm Short!" Then with her lips pulled back and her teeth clenched in rage she pulls down so hard, his knees hit the floor as his mouth flies open in something between a gulp and a yelp. "I'm Fat!" With his eyes only inches from hers, she viciously twists his balls saying, "And I'm Proud of That!"

His bulging eyes speak of the unholy pain he is suffering as he just moans on his knees in front of her begging, "Please for the love of money lady! Please let go! I'll do anything you say, just don't pull off the jewels."

Having his head now at the perfect level for a viciously swiping backhand she releases his balls just as she slaps him hard enough to knock him back, falling flat on his back. "Get out of my sight lout! Or next time I'll feed you those balls off a skewer."

The room snickers trying hard not to laugh too much as he crawls off groaning with one hand tucked between his thighs. Dovey watches him go frowning as he crawls away but casually she reaches over to snag a meatball or two on tiny skewers sucking on one as she responds, "Now where is Pepper's cooking, I really need it?"

I make a note to self to tell Pepper about the scene and that exact statement the next time I see her. Turning to commiserate with Hex, "Being away from home makes it very easy to want to be back at Mistress's house but what is being done must be done. The food Pepper makes is so much better and more varied not to mention that Mistress has a much better tub than this, hers has warmer water that has a pleasant fragrance as well as being blue green and feeling slicker."

Hex smiles and explains, "The water for Mistress's hot tub comes from deep in the earth, it was Mistress that first had me devise a method of using it. There was a small but very hot steamy crack in the floor of the room and Mistress had me do research. This slave and Crap designed a way to have water warmed there for use in both the hot tub and the kitchen. Crap has always been so good at making things, with her help we fashioned the pipes and tanks to make it all happen. Later when a book held some clues about making the 'Obscene Altars' more efficient this slave experimented with materials that had been magically enhanced, causing a nasty explosion that spread a corrosive magical dust over my body. Being stunned there was no way for me to escape from the rubble. But Toy and Crap dug me out and carried me to the tub in time for the healing properties of the water to save everything but the hair this slave once grew."

She smiles to herself in recollection, "Mistress was not pleased with the mess but her first question was to wonder if the dust could be used to make a beauty aid that the house could sell. Mistress had been getting tired of Toy shaving in the tub so wanted a powder that would keep us from having to sharpen the curved blades."

On hearing Toy's name I cringe a little knowing that my actions were responsible for her not being with us but looking to Hex I see only concern in her eyes. "I really did not mean to cast the spell, I just did not dream I could but when it happened it just slipped out of me."

Hex frowns, "Much of that blame lies with this sorry slave. It was her duty to have you more prepared. You never understood what was happening this slave should have discovered that you were more capable." Leaning close so only I can hear her whisper, "When we return we must find out more about this gift that enables you and Mistress to share so much. We should also discover why this has happened and how it can be used to the best advantage. This slave saw her pain when the lash touched you, but then also saw it stop even though yours continued. This is a rare thing and this Hex is always drawn to study rare things."

Wallowing in self-pity, I am not to be side tracked, "But Toy is not with the household she is a sister and is missed badly. She is so bright and happy she brings joy to everyone. She was always the one who was so pretty and had clothes so perfect. This girl feels like the world is a duller drabber place without her."

"Sister sweetest, the names Mistress gives us have all had careful caring thought behind them. Mistress would never have a slave she could not name. Everyone in her house has a name which speaks not of Mistress but of the slave. Mistress takes every slave and makes them so much more. Just like you and everyone else, Mistress leaves her mark on more than our skin sister. When Mistress first found Toy she was dancing in rags yet everyone loved the dance. Mistress brought her home and taught her how to create beautiful clothes and more about dancing than most performers ever dream of forgetting."

Hex continues to explain, "Crap was a struggling artisan making knives for the market. But Mistress saw that everything Crap had made bore the quality that only a true artist who cares about what is being created can bring. She actually kidnapped her so she could teach her the hammer art."

Looking around Hex gazes with pride at the group, "Even Cum our brother was just a male whore, regularly abused by wicked women and hateful men. She rescued him, gave him a useful skill, taught him to fight and made him the finest man servant in all London. Sister, she will have her Toy back, for not even the Demigoddess herself could take one of Mistress's loves from her, so do not cry over what has happened, besides you have been told what is expected of you and why." With that history and a nod to the door, we see it swinging open as Horatio enters.

I hop to my feet and go over, reaching him I lower my head saying, "May this girl be of service, Sir?" Moving closer to him than some people would be comfortable with; I kneel before him and wait for his response.

He hesitates as if unsure what to do with me but then he reaches down gently takes hold of my upper arm pulling me up. "I need to talk to you and my clothes need folding so come to my room." He leads me away still holding my elbow. Entering his room I find that his and my clothing and armor have been returned with the rents and gashes in his plating serviceably but not elegantly repaired. I proceed to the small pile of his clothing alongside the larger pile of his armor and look up quizzically folding while waiting for whatever it is that he needs to say.

"L-last night in the t-tub, I, I, I'm sorry but that was not r-right!" He stammers. "It-it is just that that I'm n-not g-good around w-women. Y-you h-had n-no choice, y-you were ordered. I-I had drank too much."

Leaving the clothing I go to him. I place my fingers to his lips, gently touching his face while I try hard to have him look me in the eye. "Shhhh, Mistress only ordered what this slave wanted. What happened was a lovely thing and means so much to this slave and maybe to so many others." I move closer resting my head briefly on his chest. I cannot let him falter now. The very best way would be to have him take me but I need to make that happen. His hands are dangling at his sides when I reach for them pulling them behind me.

"Please Sir, you're so strong and last night was so good, this girl needs to know she is wanted. Please Sir; show her you still want her." I feel him hesitate but with my head on his chest I can hear the quickening of his heart. Releasing his hands so they lay on my ass I move my own hands to the small of his back barely tugging more just guiding his hips tighter to mine. I just murmur up as I raise my lips close to his, waiting, desperately hoping he kisses me. I have almost given up when his face relaxes and his eyes close before his lips brush then press onto mine. The intoxication of that kiss contrasts so sharply with my frustration of being seemingly pliant when I want so badly simply to tear his robe off and drag him back on top of me.

He picks me up and carries me to the bed, laying me down gently never breaking the kiss. He is immensely strong with rippling muscles as hard as wrapped wire. I raise my hands to hold him, to pull him down on top of me. But I cannot hurry him he is far too strong; I can only welcome his weight when I eventually feel him crush me to the bed. I am so ready for him now; the dampness on my thighs is evident. I lift my legs and wrap them around him, hooking my heels behind his waist as I desperately pull at the towel trying to free it. His robe falls to the side of us leaving only the towel as the barrier between him and I, he swiftly yanks the offending item away. Partly standing leaning over me he reaches out and almost shyly touches my breast tracing the words of my bond and carefully avoiding my pierced nipple. But I smile up at him placing my hand over his and pressing hard into my breast. His eyes seem to bulge a bit as the fingers of my other hand grab at his lovely ass pulling him closer bringing my hips up and rubbing my clit and rings over the helm of his cock.

He gives a low moan and with the strength and conviction of a paladin plunges his penis into me with a powerful thrust. His thrust had hurt but oh so nicely, it has driven my shoulders back and down into the bed. He partly withdraws to drill me again but this time I use the leverage I have on his back to keep my hips high in the air as he plunges his cock deeper filling me completely as he comes down. With my legs around his waist like a vice I moan as I feel his whole being inside me. A warm fire runs from deep in my core and grows to rage through my body consuming me as again and again we thrust back and forth each time crashing into my essence. I close my eyes; I can hear his panting, feel his hot breath on me as he thrusts, now harder and faster. Hanging on like a limpet around his waist I scream,

"Don't stop! Don't ever stop!" My blood is thundering through my body, the whole world seeming to compress into a tight ball of just him and me. I am him; he is me, there is nothing else. That instant comes as we both erupt. It comes like Mistress's lash had come, hard brutally binding us together for just an instant, an instant where we both fall into each other completely. Both of us giving and taking as we explode. Both of us feel what the other feels. I feel his sweet fire burning up through the core of his cock to erupt in volcanic splendor as I clench myself around him. I know he feels my own wildly raging eruption as his cock thrusts deeply filling and thrilling me totally. We both spasm into splendor until with one last shudder he clings hard to me before falling back to one side lying on his back.

Panting with sweat glistening on his entire body he gasps, "Doll I am very inexperienced b-but what was that? Did you cast some sort of Succi spell on me?"

In wonder I reply, "No, No Sir that was not a spell! This slave can only cast heal or seduce. She would only heal if you needed and would never dare to seduce you. But this slave can feel and sometimes share her feelings with others. This girl felt you all the way inside her and wanted to be more with you so shared what she was feeling. Was she wrong Sir? It was for you, not against you." I had not thought my actions through, now I have to find a way for him to understand that this was not immoral. I can not tell him everything but I may be able to open the window a bit if only to become even more special to him.

He looked at me strangely, "I have been with a few women who wanted only to rise higher within the ranks of our order. But I have never communed with another like this. You truly are doll like but a doll with a rare gift. I'm going to have to ask your Mistress about you even though she made herself clear already."

He wants to buy me! He wants me to be his alone, he still does not understand. I sigh in resignation maybe Mistress will talk some sense into him, I really hope so for I know deep in her heart Mistress would sooner give up both legs than one of her family.

Chapter Seventeen

Even though there has been no word of my sister, the sweet assassin or her quest, I have to believe that no news is good news. Not wanting to spend any more time worrying about something I cannot control I have taken Boyo and Slut for a morning stroll, both are on their knees and now they actually seem to enjoy this, trying to see who can be the best pet. I love to see them like this; they are starting to bond as companion slaves quite well. But looking around at the others in the streets I am seeing far too many nobles for this early in the morning. We demons do not actually need sleep but a great many of my more self-indulgent contemporaries seem to enjoy relaxing perhaps a bit too much. I can't help but wonder why there are so many and why we all seem to be going in the same direction. There must be several dozen nobles and even more gentry about. Shrugging my natural paranoia off, I can at least rest assured that there will not be an Inq intrusion in this area. But as I turn the corner I see nine of the top ten ranking Succi Demons in all of hell chatting to the three ranking Inq demons. Something smells really bad and I do not think it is just the sulfur. In the hierarchy of hell my place should be number seven in that rank, the fact that the rest of the members of Council of Ten are here and I had not been call upon is not just a little unsettling. I feel a shiver of premonition run up my spine just as my Slut recognizes what is in front of us.

I am motioned forward my apprehensions realized, somehow this gathering is about me. Stepping to them boldly and shortening my hold on my slave's leashes, "Is there a problem here?" I ask.

"Nothing that cannot be dealt with, one way or another but perhaps challenge is a better term for what is before us all." Was the response from the ranking Inq, someone I am not subject to!

Looking around smiling with the oiliest of smiles I have seen in years! Another continues, "You seem to have developed a preference for enslaving Inquisitors and I find that disturbing. So I have come here in good faith to better understand this." This from the Inquisitor Prince, DeSkyz. I hold no allegiance to him either, quite the opposite. I turn to him scornfully looking him up and down, I can almost feel my hackles rise as I respond forcefully, "Those I have taken were taken in honorable combat after they attacked the house of Mistress Copper. I now hold their collar and leashes!" As I reach down to stroke Slut's hair I growl, "And your problem is? They are MINE and nothing in that is 'negotiable'."

He speaks deliberately and in an insulting way as he smarms at me. "I see no brands. The leashes you hold have little worth without a brand to cement the bond; I would be prepared to offer you a good settlement for you to return them to me."

I'm starting to get really angry but I know that he is only trying to bait me into a stupid move so I turn to him and merely smile, "I never sell MINE but might consider a trade." I take a step forward; reach out and almost touching his throat. "I would free these two perhaps for your leash but I shall never sell them."

He only growls, "You are too much like your Mistress! You're still a slave at heart. You even still wear her brand. Although perhaps it is because you refuse to bear the pain of removing the brand that you still display her marks?"

I snarl at him in open challenge then, which startled him a little but not enough to keep him from continuing. "But no I had a different currency in mind." He puts his finger to his chin in a theatrical show of pretending to think purses his lips and continues. "I was actually thinking of another, I was thinking of someone who has recently fallen into extreme disfavor in London; I believe you know him, Malthus?"

I feel the impact of his words like a fist rammed into my belly. I can not help but gnash my teeth at the sound of the hated name. I bare my fangs and cannot control my tail as it whips from side to side. Glaring at his gloating face I feel the desperate need to punch my talons through his eyes or throat. My rage is so apparent to all that although I never said a word the Inquisitor Prince of hell involuntarily takes three steps back saying, "I came here in good faith! Someone control that bitch."

I am so angry I will not even talk. I go over to the brazier burning at the side of the plaza and stick the talon of my index finger in. I look down to my slaves. I grind my teeth together and focus myself. "You have permission to beg for my brand now MINE."

Boyo is fastest as he raises himself off of all fours to kneel with knees spread before me, "Please Mistress this slave begs for your brand, he shall forever be naked without it."

I turn to his sister slave saying, "Kneel and watch carefully." Dropping both leashes to the ground and stepping on Slut's, I grab his horns and spin him around forcing him back to all fours again. I use my talon now heated to a branding temperature and carve into his left buttock 'MINE'. His screams echo through the plaza we are in; Demons and Demonesses smile

171

and point, the Inquisitor Demons frown and start to move forward as if to intervene but are stopped by the mightiest of us all. I thrust my finger back into the brazier and look at Slut. I don't smile; I will not brand her if she does not beg. But either way her life will never be the same again. She is smart enough to know not only, what I want her to say but that I will never ask her to say it.

Head lowered, eyes to the ground as she kneels before me she speaks clearly and loudly enough for the three Inquisitors to hear,

"This girl offers her submission to you Mistress!" are the first words she speaks.

"This girl offers her submission to you Mistress!" She repeats louder

"This girl offers her submission to you Mistress!" She almost screams. I feel the bonding complete.

"This slave earnestly begs to have your mark burned into her flesh Mistress! Please Mistress this slave begs for this mercy!"

I never utter a single word but spin her around violently and start to carve the four letter word deep and bold, causing the up rushing of blood to outline each letter, I start with the 'M'. My slave Slut never screams, she grits her teeth breathing, "Thank you!"

The next letter 'I' is etched into her flesh while she yells out, "Thank You!'

I reheat my talon in the fire to continue with the 'N'. After it she screams to the heavens, "Thank You!"

Finally with a flourish I end with the last letter 'E' searing it into her flesh as she proclaims to all and looks directly at the group of Inquisitors,

"Thank You!"

With every letter I felt the bond strengthen until at the end of the last letter it is sealed and she is weeping softly.

I turn growl and walk over to the prince. "I have taken these! They are now MINE! Now since you know my Mistress so well let me quote her to you, for yes she is the Mistress of my heart. 'Once MINE, always MINE!' Those are her words and her credo. She taught me to believe in them and now they are also mine. And as for that pig called, Malthus I would not have him, I'll leave him for one of yours to cut apart." I turn my back on him deliberately, first because it is an insult but secondly because I am so angry I feel tears coming to my eyes. I can only grab the leashes of MINE and cast to transport us to another plane, one with a good bar I know.

Just standing there shaking I release the leashes, "Go get me the strongest vilest drink they have, I'll find me a place out of the way to drown in it." When both have gone as ordered I take out the Hell-phone and call Mistress telling her about the nobility of hell trying to trade the freedom and soul of Malthus. The change in her voice is very noticeable and not one of jubilation. "He has been isolated from his own people? Wonderful, I'm not even sure his spells will work anymore. But be advised he is still a deadly enemy and a rat in a trap is even more likely to tear your fingers off if you are not careful. Now I am forewarned my sweet but that is just one of the strange events happening. Your sister Doll seems to have very nicely attracted the amorous attentions of the new Inquisitor General who appears to be a young but very reasonable gentleman. Also to recover the Crystal Chalice there was a battle like I have never seen or even heard of in all my years. By my best guess, more than several thousand of the beastlings died trying to prevent us from getting that cup. I can only surmise that there is a game afoot, and someone has very smelly feet."

Chapter Eighteen

I had been with Horatio most of the day just basking in our warm afterglows and his arousing male essence as well as frequently stirring his hot blooded ardor. It had been lovely just him and I talking about his life in Oxford, learning under Thomas and training to be a warrior priest. I learned that Thomas had not let Malthus know of the levels of prowess Horatio had achieved. I told him of Mistress, how she loved and guided us and how we all worked together to achieve her goals. I also explained her fierce pride of those she called MINE. I even hinted at how the brand had bound me to her. But this was all spaced between several more explorations that led to trying new positions and teaching Horatio more about how to give me pleasure, something he has readily committed to do. Each time just in the moment before we came I reached out mentally to feel him so that we could both experience what each other was feeling. His amazement at this was almost embarrassing but after first being startled, his compliments were very sweet.

There is a faint knocking on the door as it swings open revealing Taken with a bemused smile on her face. She makes no comment as she takes in the view of the two of us sprawled naked and entwined on the bed. "Mistress wants to continue with the quest as soon as she can. This slave has been told to bring you both back as Mistress needs to talk to us all before everyone leaves on the next part of the quest. She also said that haste may be in order so you had better grab some food to eat while we travel."

I jump up and get myself clean before hastily donning my armor; Horatio does not seem to be in the same hurry so I am able to help him strap the last of his armor on before he leaves. Alone I do a detailed check of the room to make sure we leave nothing but our sweet and passionate karma in the room. I need to make sure everything is left properly, Mistress has assigned me as an aide, well maybe more than just an aide but I will get all parts of the job right. Minutes later I emerge into the common area joining the others in the party with Mistress standing in front.

"We are all here now so I only have to say this once and as most of you know I'm not fond of repeating myself. Yesterday we were obviously expected, the traps and the number of the beastlings were a sign that someone really does not want us to complete this quest. I have no idea who that might be as both Demigods have helped and encouraged us. That is the bad news. The good news is that we may not have the same opposition today. The information about where we are going is in language only used by a few scholars like Thomas, Lillith and one of my own." I see my sister Hex give a small smile and proudly lift her head. "This may and I hope it does mean that we hopefully have stolen a march on who ever set up those disasters yesterday. We know the nightingale was there, even though Doll killed that one, it tells us that we were being watched. I had thought that they were pets of Malthus but now I'm not so sure."

Horatio steps forward, "No not Malthus it is well known in our ranks that he has had an irrational fear of all birds especially night birds for years. He even gave orders to the new recruits to clear nests out of Oxford every spring. So Inquisitors are definitely not to blame for this and that I will give my word on."

"Thank you for that confirmation, I do not presume to doubt your word Inquisitor General; I merely stated what I had believed. There is a mystery here and I'm not sure either you or I are going to like the answers we find. But that is not my point, from now on, No One will say out loud any information on our destinations. I say this because if there are eyes watching us there may very well be ears hearing us as well. So form up we have a march to begin and a quest to complete."

With Mistress's words echoing in our hearts we set off through the caverns of the catacombs but this time we were leaving. I see only one beastling who dies under the blast of my partially recharged wand. There are nowhere near the number in evidence that had been here before. I revel in the thought that our band may have actually reduced the number of beastlings in these catacombs by so many. We carry on, me in the lead again with Dovey and Slice directing me, Mistress is behind chatting with Horatio and Hex. I must try hard not to think about the conversations they might be having, I have a job to do and I'm going to do it right. I let my senses out trying to feel again, immediately I turn and fire, killing another of those horrible spying birds. Mistress goes over with Hex and Horatio and stirs in the carcass with the tip of her silver dagger, finally she fishes out the golden metal and ceramic piece that Hex has come to associate with the birds spying. I don't know how Hex got so smart but I do trust that if she says something, it is correct. I only know that the birds feel somehow wrong; they make my skin turn cold, clammy and itchy, almost like you feel just before you break into a cold sweat. I also know killing them is easy and feels both refreshing and cleansing sort of like when you have just washed your face. I wait until they are back in line and notice that Horatio's jaw is set in a hard almost cruel expression I have never seen before, he looks like he wants to kill someone, I am glad it is not me. Ahh, at last, there directly ahead is the crack in the wall we had entered by.

Starting to press through the crack I hear a single in-drawn breath and see a shadow flit across the edge of my vision. Reflexively I pull back just in time to see a curved blade slash where my throat had been. I don't wait for the beat of my own heart. I dive forward through the opening rolling and landing on the other side of the wall and come up facing back to the crack, level my wand and fire blazing the attacker on the right. Slice jumps through the opening next slashing at the other on the left then everything stops for me. There is a burning impact on my back; I seem to be moving in slow motion. Falling forward I feel a scream of pain bite through my back and looking down I see the mail below my breast pushed outwards with the bloody tip of a dagger jutting out. The pain spasm into a spike of agony as the dagger is withdrawn causing my blood to geyser freely out from the deep wounds. I cough blood, taste copper as I land face first in a widening pool of my own blood. Everything has slowed and I see Cyril in slow motion come through the wall; I hear him scream as though from very far away, "Help her!"

As if I am a distant observer, I witness a war whip slash through a hand holding a knife that would have killed Cyril. There is Horatio impaling a foe on his blade then looking back at me. Our eyes meet, he let's go of his blade, clasping his hands together as a cold force races between us. My body bucks hard as the healing forces course through me. I can feel the energy gathering inside me as the icy cold healing seers through the wound. I cough once spattering blood with my breath; I can breathe again and the world is coming back into focus. Rolling over beside the corpse of the ugly that had attacked me, I see my blood on his blade. Everyone is through the crack in the wall now and they have killed or wounded all but a few. There are maybe twenty bodies on the ground as both Mistress and Horatio come over to me.

Mistress reaches out and slaps my face in suppressed anger tinged with fear, "You almost died MINE! That is simply not good enough! I don't want you to try anything as stupid as that again! You are far too valuable to me alive! You are not a heavily armored warrior; you are lightly armored with a long range weapon. Now tell me just what part of LOOOONG RAAANGE don't you understand. A scout uses her head or she lose s her head, it is that simple. You never should have gone through that opening first. I know that you knew there was danger there but you jumped into a fight that should have been Slice's. Because of you Cyril was almost killed as well. As it is Horatio had to stop fighting and risk himself to cast the heal that saved your life."

I understand exactly what is happening. Mistress is really angry but she is angry for me not at me. All I can do is, kneel in front of her, try not to cry and wait until her berating lessens. It feels terrible to be punished for stupidity especially in front of those you had put at risk but I endure Mistress's tirade recognizing the worry and concern that accompanies it until I suddenly become aware of the spying bird. Mistress knows immediately what I have felt and looks directly into my eyes with a very slight nod. She put her hand on my collar to pull me up saying very loudly, "You better mind your place girl I have you on point for a reason. Now let us all be off to the dungeons of SoHo."

With a shove she pushes me forward through the exit into the underground Station. As I pass through the doorway I feel the presence of the bird fade as Mistress whispers to Dovey, "We still need to have the same route that was just a bit of misdirection back there." Dovey nods smiling and points to the green arrow that will take us to Piccadilly station directly away from the SoHo district. We move quickly through the underground almost racing now until we emerge into the streets outside of Cutty Sark Station, the very district of London we call home. Going south then east for a long way before heading south again we enter into the outer courtyard of the

National Maritime Museum. Mistress looks at me raising an eyebrow. Her concern I know is now for spies so, with that in mind I reach out trying to feel once move but find nothing. I look back at her shaking my head, no.

"The directions we were given were in two parts, the first read, 'Pass by seven open ports of call before following a star through the opening' the second part instructed us to, 'Lift the weight of seven stones at the seventh stone'. This seems to me to be a lot of gibberish like code and because it was written in a language long dead this may take a whileso let's see what there is to see." Finally, while looking pointedly at me, "No one is to take foolish chances we all need to work together now."

I wince at Mistress's words knowing this is one more reminder of my foolishness but Horatio smiles at me reassuringly as once more I take the lead. Before me are a set of high double doors, I sense nothing amiss rather the opposite as if this is a place of ancient strength and forbearance. As I press forward one of the doors opens effortlessly into a large room with many display cases showing odd hardware and artifacts with small written legends that attract the devoted attentions of both Hex and Crap. There are many small doors all closed including one directly in front of us but to the left there is an arched portal surrounded by sculptured stone work, this portal holds no door or door jamb. Mistress Copper looks at the opening, taps Hex on the shoulder to get her attention away from the display cases she is poring over and holds up a finger symbolizing one triumphantly.

I hurry on to the door in front of us, thankfully the door opens without a trap being sprung and I see before me a room like the last but with only a single door directly in before of us. I have a real sense of urgency now, it appears Mistress maybe correct in her thoughts about stealing the march on whoever is trying to stop us, but I don't know how long that will hold. I silently motion for everyone to follow us and hurry to the next doorway.

Again no traps I am almost elated especially when I see another open archway to our left.

I clearly hear Hex speaking softly to Mistress as we cross the room, "Ahh Mistress I understand it now. This is a museum of all things nautical. When boats mattered to all the world the word, 'Port' was a word meaning the left side or the side of the boat to the port while "Starboard' meant right or out to the sea of stars. So 'Pass by seven open ports of call before following a star through the opening' means passing seven openings or archways to the left before going through the opening to the right. Five more archways then we turn right and go through. I'm not sure about the stone reference yet, but I remember now that it was once a measure of weight."

I don't know all the things that Hex does but if I have to find five more arches on the left I am not going to stand around talking about it. I run to the next doorway and then the next keeping on going until I have seen all seven archways. Looking around for the first time there is an arch on the right. We all head quickly over to look into the opening and see it is different from in every other room there. On the floor of all the other rooms had been close fitting tile but here there are large flat stones that are lose ly fitted together with a mortar.

I walk straight forward counting and stand on the seventh stone turning around to smile at Mistress saying, "Here Mistress, this must be the place." Stepping aside Cum, Slice and Horatio take out their daggers and start chipping away at the mortar between the stones. I can see their surprise at what they find for it readily becomes apparent that while the rest of the stones seem to be thin this once is many, many times thicker.

The rest of us take a much needed break eating and drinking some of our supplies. I feel my energy start to come back to me, I had not realized just how much I needed to eat but now I eat voraciously. I understand that I need to replace what has been lost in the healing. To finish Dovey hands me a small flask and taking a small sip of the fiery liquor I let it warm me from the inside.

Cum finally lifts one of the stones beside the mammoth one free, allowing them to dig down beside it and displaying a large flat stone that is fully a foot thick. Enlarging the hole by removing another three stones then digging down on three sides enables them to gain a purchase and with a mighty heave from all three they roll the stone out exposing a lid of a box buried beneath the stone. Hex automatically goes over to check for traps and when satisfied that it is safe steps aside, after that forcing it open proves an easy task for them as they use their swords to pry the lid free. In the box rests a large bell with many deeply incised lines running both vertically and horizontally across its surface. There is also a thin gold sheet that has lines and words forced into it. This gold leaf sheet is automatically handed to Hex.

Her face lights up saying, "Mistress, a map!", then seriously warning. "The map tells how to get to the Skeleton King but warns that the bell may only be rung once and only at his command. That bell must carry a powerful set of spells for it says here that if even tapped gently it will explode and kill everyone close by. But Mistress the location, it appears to be very close maybe two hours walk from here to the entrance of an underground maze. Truly this is our key as it also directs us how to get through the maze."

Mistress seems pleased at the news but finally asks the question that had been nagging at all of us. "Does it perhaps tell of how my Sugar is going to give a skeleton head? For by my eyes taking those candles would seem to be the stealing Sugar had needed to accomplish."

Hex merely shakes her head and shows the map to Dovey. "Oh I know of this place it was once called Veralaneum and is older than old. But if we are going to make it before dark we had better get going, we just can't take the time to repair this floor. So lead on Doll we have ground to cover." She hands me the map and points out the route we will have to travel. "If we take the streets south from here then go directly through the forest we can cover ground fastest so take us this way my dear and we will make it before dark."

She does not have to remind me that I'd better be more careful and keep a watchful eye for the bird spies. I commit the map to memory by picturing it in my mind, thinking of something else then bringing the picture back and comparing it to the map. Satisfied that I can remember the route I hand it back to her. As we are making our way out Mistress has to prompt both Hex and Crap to hurry even going so far as to promise them she would make time to bring them back here after the quest. I try to keep moving as fast as I can as we break out into the late afternoon sunlight; I have my route and press on without even looking backwards setting a pace that I worry may strain Dovey. Soon streets give way to the forest making it easier to make my way down the cool pathways through the fragrant green trees. As I finally lead the party into a small village I spy the inn that was indicated on the map. This is supposed to be the entrance to an underground maze. On entering all seems rather conventional, a somewhat small unobtrusive bar with an affable looking barkeep of more than ample proportions waiting.

"And how can I serve you on this fine day?" While the question was expected it is quickly brushed aside by Mistress.

Mistress merely walked over takes out a large gold covered coin and asked, "Your maze, where is the entrance? I need to know now."

His only response is to sigh, "Too few who go in come out again, actually in my lifetime not one person has returned. I'd rather serve you some food and ale than doom you to eternity in that warren but gold is gold." He first holds out his hand for the coin and on receiving it walks to the wall rolls back a salacious tapestry only a Succi could truly appreciate and exposes a barred doorway. "There is a pull cord on the inside that will ring this bell not that I have ever heard it ring. The door I keep barred at all times, my father and grandfather have told me of undead that live below. I have only known five people to go in and they did not return. So I wish you well but if you want to leave any more coin it would probably be best as I doubt you will ever have need of it again."

Horatio's sword all of a sudden is under the barkeep's chin. "We would perhaps be more partial to increase our generosity after we return but while Mistress Copper's purse has funded all our endeavors so far, it would be more fitting for me to provide you with an incentive to make sure we are not delayed from our appointed tasks any further. Now unlock the door!"

The barkeeper does not appear to be feigning shock at Horatio's not too subtle menacing threats, "Just joking", and quickly reaches up take down a key keeping a close eye on Horatio's sword, turns it in the lock to free the bars.

Chapter Nineteen

I brush by the barkeeper not giving him a second thought but rather concentrating my whole being on feeling, listening, seeing and smelling what is ahead of us. Holding the gold leaf map in my left hand and my wand in my right enables me to reference either as needed as we proceed forward. The place is as silent as a grave, a corridor of only about four feet in width with smooth stone above, below and to either side. The pallid grey stonework appearing unmarked by any tool is as smooth as a freshly shaved leg; the slippery smooth surface partly reflects the light from the lanterns, making seeing ahead very easy. The air is humid but not musty rather there seems to be a cool gentle breeze brushing feather like fingertips on my face. I can sense nothing hostile, no unseen lurkers seeking to spy on us. The corridor seems to go on forever in a straight line but the map indicates that some distance ahead there is a tee and we are to go to the right.

In the far distance I can barely discern movement and lights with figures behind. Holding my hand up to stop everyone I rest my wand on the floor then take the lantern from Dovey and move it in a circle and see the distant lantern moving exactly as the one I am holding. Smiling I hand the lantern back and pick up my wand moving ahead with more confidence seeing our reflections grow rapidly at the end of the hallway.

As I enter the junction as shown on the map I know it's there but can still hardly see it. Turning the corner I point to the right and Dovey shines the light down the corridor. Gasping in fright I see ahead perhaps thirty skeletal warriors in full armor with blades in hand. There is an instant of panic before I bring my weapon to bear but in that instant the totally unexpected occurs, every single skeleton goes down on one knee with the tip of its sword resting on the stone floor. Every single one of them bows their heads to me.

"Uhh Mistress you must see this!" Are the only words I can get past my lips! This is just too strange! We have cut and hacked our way through literally thousands of uglies and undead to get this far and now skeletons are kneeling almost in silent homage to us. I just cannot believe my eyes.

"Now this is not what I had expected! Doll I want you to be very careful, do not attack unless attacked but we still have to get through them." Then Mistress whispers to me, "Can you feel anything?"

I just shake my head saying softly, "Nothing at all Mistress." I'm quaking in my boots as I take my first steps towards them; oh right, I'm not wearing boots, well shaking in my sandals or whatever, I'm scared! My heart is thudding so loud that I'm sure everyone can hear it as I tentatively step forward. Those directly in front of me shift to the side to let me pass allowing just enough room for us all to go through single file occasionally brushing their cold bones as we go. We all pass without incident but as Crap and Taken, the rear guard of the party move past, the skeletons as one stand, turn, sheath their weapons and follow perhaps fifteen feet behind. The noise they make is like dry twigs rubbing on each other, a dry crackling sound almost husky in its tone. They have no smell and I have no intention of touching any of them again. But they do not seem in anyway hostile rather they behave more like an honor guard. I have no idea why this is happening but at the next corner we meet yet another cohort of these boney fingered warriors. I count fifty-five turnings that we make in this maze and each and every time we are met by another thirty of the warriors. This is an army of undead; I am starting to believe the correctness of the name the Skelton King for surely only a king could command so many warriors. The fifty fifth turning leads us to a set of double doors with another group of skeleton warriors, this time larger than the rest, the front rank having long pole weapons while the rear have menacing looking wands. But these too part for us and actually pull the two huge double doors open revealing a large well lit throne room beyond. There sitting on a throne of skulls is a skeleton dressed in rich brocaded purple and green robes and crowned with a circlet of vine and flowers.

I know this is a step for me to take but I had recently rushed in too soon, however looking around it is easy to tell that there are more swords outside the room than in. As we enter he nods politely to each of us.

I am aghast when he stands and beckons me over. I hear words in my mind, but also see his jaw move in a parody of speech. "Believe it or not, you all have just earned my undying gratitude. So please come in, we have quite a lot of business to attend to as well as some explanations for you all. Fear not my guard, for the gold leaf you carry guarantees free and honored passage in the halls of my fortress. Anything else would result in a very desperate battle for your lives. But please come in, it has been a long time since I have heard a voice from a human throat."

Looking around he locates Sugar and strides directly over to her personally greeting her by bowing low saying, "You, who walks with death have been ordained to give me back my life, I thank you. For that great gift you bring me, I have crafted a tool of your trade so please allow me give you a gift."

Sugar like all of us just looks up in awe and amazement, grabbing her throat she just nods to him in stunned silence. He turns to a doorway as it opens admitting a skeleton bearing a cushion covered with a cloth. Taking the cushion from the skeletal servitor he uncovers it revealing a pair of small triple bladed trident like knives that he presents to Sugar. Taking them she holds one up in admiration demonstrating that the long center blade ending in a vicious point changes, for if it is turned in one direction it has the same sheen as a silver dagger but turn it the other way and the second side is the black light sucking metal of a demon blade. Where the crossbar would have been is a rod that curves up on either side extending fully two thirds of the length of the central dual sided blade. Both of these rods have the outer edges sharpened. The sculpted hilts of the matching knives are pure black and shaped to comfortably fit a small hand. "I'm sure my dear that you shall make great use of these."

Sugar looks at the multi-purpose knives again in admiration everyone can see just how exquisite they are. She drops to one knee and with one hand on her throat, squeaks out, "Thank you your highness."

It is then that he turns to Cyril, with his first glance at him there is an eerie radiance that begins to seep out from where his eyes must once have been. "This is another one I shall be gifting today, come here lad your destiny awaits you." Turning back to the throne and sitting, words continue to emanate from him even though he does not actually speak but rather broadcasts his thoughts. "Before I can give you your due, I must ask you to remove your shirt lad; I need to see your chest to make sure it is you I can give this to. Many events have gone into this meeting and many people have tried and failed to get this far but the balance is about to be regained so please, remove your shirt."

Cyril looks extremely puzzled and glances longingly back at the doorways close to panic, but then visibly stealing himself he steps to the front and removes his shirt revealing his tattoos. With this display the Skeleton King reaches back and pulls a tapestry to the ground. What the tapestry has been hiding is a painting carved into the smooth pallid stone.

The paint gives color to the carved shapes, shapes of vines, lilies and doves all both dead and alive with the words etched above "Love Over All". The wall painting is an exact match to the tattoos on Cyril's chest.

There in that second frozen forever in my memory; there in that second while we stand in the halls of the Skeleton King, every fleshy jaw drops open. "This painting has been here for over 300 years just as the scroll that carries the quest has been lost many times over the years as well. Many have tried to find their way here and with each there has been one needing the regenerative healing only I can give and another bearing this image. All but you have failed; but you need to know why if you are to survive. But first, let me give the second gift. Felicity Copper you are the 'Mistress of the Whip', mortal leader of the cult of the Succubus. Horatio Duncannon you are the 'Inquisitor General' of all the cult of the Inquisitors. It is time you meet he who will be 'The High Druid' of the Druidic cult of these lands. Cyril Cllywn you have been destined to receive this, the second Druidic spell book, I have the first. For as Lillith and Thomas, my old companions are the spiritual leaders of their cults, it is I, Creighton who shall hold the post of Demigod for all druids. Come accept your spell book now. It holds several useful spells that you will be able to use as long as you merely carry this mistletoe with you."

Cyril almost in a trance steps forward and takes a leather bag in one hand and a wooden bound book in the other. He looks up at the seated boney figure and nods to him. He opens the book and just stares; he turns first one then another page before closing the book with a snap. Attempting to pass it back to the King he pleads, "This is not for me, it would take more courage than I possess to even contemplate casting some of these spells. Take it back please; I'm not a doer of great deeds just a poor thief who hides from his shadow."

The Skeleton King makes no move to take it but there is a dry rattle that might have once been the echo of a chuckle, "No coward could have traveled the road you have taken even in such august company. After you return to London you shall divide your time between the forests close to here and to the tutelage of my soon to be savior Sugar."

Looking away from Cyril dismissively he looks over at Mistress, "There is one other here who must now receive a gift. Mistress Copper, do I have your permission to give your Doll a gift which will help her today, a gift that will sharpen her unique ability that can be of use to us all in our goal?"

With a nod Mistress presses me forward towards the Skeleton King who reaches once more behind himself and takes out a small box. Handing the box to me he instructs, "The ability that came with your brand has been searching for someone that could wear it for many years. Those who in the past have found themselves with that ability were all killed before it could be used. The medallion on this necklace will enhance the ability far beyond what it is now, as well as provide a protective barrier around you. So put it on now, you are going to need it."

He turns to the group as a whole and intones, "Long ago there were three of us and by a manic misadventures you may learn of later we all three became immortal. But to allow two to escape an eternal torment I stayed behind while they went on. But for this mercy, my flesh was eaten from my body. I was chained, immortal, but fully able to feel pain while piece by piece of my flesh fell to the teeth and claws of a truly foul creature. That creature also gained immortality from my flesh and lives today; that is the creature controlling the birds your scout Doll can kill. She also controls and directs the robotic police force. She is the true enemy of all mankind and all mankind must unite to free themselves from her damning clutches. But I digress, I have so much to tell you and so little time, the ritual must be completed shortly while the energies of this world pulse fast this night. To fail now would mean waiting another year."

He steps away from the throne, what he has already said is completely out of my realm but Mistress, Horatio and Hex are huddled together whispering almost as one. He goes to a central part of the room where the stone seemed to be slightly sunken, turns to us and prescribes, "Sugar will need four to assist her, Cyril, Horatio, Felicity and the empath Doll. You four must hold the lit candles and have them melt into the cup held by Sugar. Doll must feel all six of us as she has never felt anyone before and bring us all into harmony. Now! Come to me with the candles and cup, for when the cup is full it must be Sugar who pours it over me and I who ring the bell." Mistress comes forward and from her pack takes the four candles, each several inches thick and several feet long. She passes one to each of us before she takes out the Crystal Chalice for Sugar and the bell for the King; finally almost as an afterthought she places three crystal skulls at his feet. I can feel the weight of the candle passed to me and hear once more the words that speak directly in our minds.

"You will need to fill and refill the Chalice as many times as it takes to completely melt the candles. These candles burn slowly, so you five will all have to have spells cast on you to increase your strength and endurance for this is a long and arduous task before us. Someone also make sure that Doll does not fall for she will not really be with the rest of us."

I feel a surge of energy course through my body, Taken comes forward and lights the candles as the white boned Skelton king sits cross legged on the floor in the depression. I reach out feeling for the other five. I can feel them all gently in my mind: Mistress caring and controlled, Horatio strong and righteous who is starting to fall in love with me, Cyril caught in a state of controlled panic wondering what he has done to deserve all this, and Sugar caring and loving but with a deep cold part of her that is a shut door. I touch the mind of the Skeleton King himself. Old sufferings burn like fire; his whole body seems held together by pain. The pain is old he has worn it like a robe for centuries, unsleeping, ever needing to scream in sheer agony. I almost cannot hold the link between us, his pain washes over us, through us, and I am the channel. Everyone shares his pain as he takes on every hurt, every fear, our loves, our hates and in return baptizes us all in his pain. I can no longer see, hear, or feel. My whole world is caught in the burning fire of his pain and every emotion we all have in us. I cannot feel my body at all; it is as if I am no longer there. All that exists for me is the link binding six of us in a raging fire. I know it is my job to hold the candle but I cannot feel my hands. I lose track of time, but not of what is happening. I can see myself through five sets of eyes holding the candle that slowly melts, filling and refilling the chalice. Each time it is full Sugar pours the wax over the head of the Skeleton King. Slowly as the wax cools on his head and body features start to appear. The more that the wax builds up on his body the less he feels that soul searing pain. It is then that I begin to feel something more than just pain. The world becomes etched around me. I feel myself become hard and brittle. I become something else other than what I have been. I am hard metal that has been scored from without and within. I am now brass itself, a bell hanging from the waxy hand of a man likething. I know what he wants now. The pain is gone but he needs us all to be in harmony. So I merge that which each of us recently held most dear, taking that single emotion the happiness each of us has felt with the going of his pain. This I merge all of it together so that as he strikes me, I ring in a single pure note before I shatter into 10,000 tiny fragments.

Slowly I become aware once more, lying in the arms of Mistress while Horatio hovers over like a mother hen. I look to the place where there had been a skeletal figure and now stands a tall naked man wearing a crown of vines. His skin, pale white covers a body fleshed and well-muscled. We all witness the pure pleasure as he runs his fingertips up his chest and holds his hands before his face. The smile he smiles is radiant, shedding joy as the sun sheds light. From the side Sugar now also smiling moves in front of him.

Her finger tips are the first woman's touch he has felt in centuries. Having attracted his attention, her fingers trace a pathway to his limpness causing that member as if in response to long a forgotten memory to twitch into awareness. With a wink and a grin Sugar's lip's move to the center of his chest and begin slowly kissing down his chest, while her now naked breasts brush and caress his cock.

Finally as his sigh, "At last!" leaves his lips, Sugar takes his member in both hands licking, kissing and finally enveloping the rapidly hardening cock in her mouth. The look on his face is one of sheer and utter rapture until very rapidly his hips spasm forward and Sugar's cheeks bulge as her mouth is filled. I look up at Mistress and feel her pride in me and her happiness for Sugar. Horatio, standing over the two of us is looking concerned but drained while Cyril looks around with a pleased but bemused expression on his face.

"Damn that was good girl, it's been over 300 years since I had one of those and all you have to do now is swallow to make those scars go away."

Sugar is all smiles as she swallows then looks up saying, "Thank you milord, so glad to accommodate you." Looking around to all of us she says excitedly, "It worked I can talk again!"

"Of course you can, such is the power of a true Druid for only we can actually restore and regenerate the flesh damaged in battle." Then as he waved to several skeletal servitors, "But before you go there is one more thing we must do before you leave. We must give the first Druidic demon her due. I shall summon the very first druidic demon ever. This demon is neither of a high nor low moral, not red nor blue, but rather the first of her kind."

The servitors have placed candles and bone white skulls in a perfect alignment over four bright green carpets, before moving a carved man-sized wooden object that hurts my eyes whenever I try to see what it is. The new

King steps to the object and begins to sing out notes that remind me of wind rushing through trees. There is a crack and a very purple demoness, very naked, looking very confused, stands there wearing one of the loveliest collars I have ever seen; the words etched on the collar are 'Spite's Slut'.

Sugar growls and grabs her knives, Taken has her sword out and the two begin to slowly advance on the Demoness. The King standing there naked raises a hand as he steps in front of them.

Mistress's cell phone goes off at that moment and Cyril moves over to the figure saying, "I have seen you before".

Everyone close to Mistress can clearly hear Spite's panicky voice on the phone followed by Mistress's answer of, "I know MINE, she is standing in front of me now and my dear you would have to see her to truly believe it but she is as purple as an amethyst. A demon forged into something we have never known or seen before. I have to deal with this now; I'll call you back just as soon as I can." Mistress clicks her phone off going forward to the Demoness. "So you are the one who started all this and with a suspicious look at the Druid King but you are also now part of my 'First Girl's' family so you will fear nothing from us, yet! Stand Down MINE! This one has been changed; she is quite obviously, no longer blue!"

The Druid King is brought a robe by a servitor and places it over his now fleshy shoulders. "Come here Spite's Slut I have something for you. Don't worry your Mistress will not be angry with you." He coaxes. "You have had your morals stripped from you. I can see that and you have the scars to prove it, later you shall have the power to remove them for soon such power will be yours. But for now you need to see your new spell book. Today in hell you can't even travel from plane to plane but with this book you shall be able to cast as long as you also keep this mistletoe with you. You are the first of your kind, you who are neither red nor blue but purple instead. It is up to you and the mortal Cyril to begin a new cult; for you are the first of the demonic druids, as he is the first mortal high druid. Your spells are now different for it will be your place to help unite the Succi's and Inq's to work and fight together against their common foe. You will foster harmony and unity, working always to help the Succi channel lust into passion and feed Inq's need to feel they have done the right thing into helping not hurting others. After so very long, the time has finally come. The time for you to look up behind me to the wall and pledge to obey that which is written there, for that is our first and last tenant. Say it with me now!"

The enslaved purple demoness looks up, her eyes had widened farther and farther with every word that the Druid King had spoken to her and Cyril. She follows, intoning with the other two the same words, "Love Over All!"

The three speak with passion in their voices and it somehow becomes musical like a chant or a hymn that they repeat three times. The Druid King with a smile, so full of joy, so bountiful and beautiful that I truly hope I remember it to my dying day, hands her the wood bound book.

"My dear would you give me your hell-phone for a minute?" He takes the phone opens it taps some keys and hands it back to her, saying, "I'm speed dial number three, which is a fitting number but now would be highly appropriate time for you to make amends to several people here."

She looks up at him in awe before she nods and turns going first to Sugar. "Please this slave begs that you accept my sincere apology for what I have done to you. She knows how much it hurt her Mistress and for that pain, this one gave up her freedom pledging to always be her slave. But for you at this time, your sister's slave can only beg forgiveness as everything belongs to Mistress already." Sugar strokes the red hair and then gently touches her face, "My own actions were rash but without my actions and yours, we would never have come to be here today so, go gently, for no assassin known to me shall ever hunt you."

Smiling with tears in her eyes she then turns to Taken, "What has happened between us before is not even an echo in the wind. You are a member of a family that Mistress placed this slave in. This slave is now a kin sister who would kill rather than see you harmed."

Finally the purple Demoness comes to me, "This slave was raised from hell to cut your heart out; it is great thing to have been part of that failure. May you walk the streets of London in peace and safety for never shall this slave allow such a thing to happen."

The Druid King then claps his hands saying, "You must return from whence you came. You need to explain to your Mistress and to study your new book. After your return, you shall give your Mistress your hell-phone so that she can talk to me and I can reassure her about what has happened here today, I will also talk about renaming you among other things." He leans over brushes his lips across her forehead then snaps his fingers and she vanished in a crack of imploding air.

Turning to us, "This maze could have been called the halls of the Skeleton King but now they will be known to all as 'The Halls of the Druid King'. Henceforth this place shall be for druids only and those seeking to be Druids. I'll have to deal with the barkeep of course but in the end the traffic coming here will fatten his purse. While honor is due you all, until there is real and pressing danger only Cyril may return. By which of course I mean that it is now time for you to leave."

Getting to my feet I still feel a bit unsteady but soon that passes. Mistress motions to the doorway and I take out the gold leaf once more. I now know how convoluted the pathway is and the maps is a very real need.

I have grown accustom to being on point and try to feel ahead but the skeletons lining the hallway are a massed single need. I can detect nothing else so just give up and try to block their single entity out. They stand to attention as we slowly pass them then escort us with an honor guard through all the hallways and fifty five turns, each time we encounter a skeleton guard they saluting us as we past until at last we come to the barred doorway where I yank hard on the pull cord to get the attention of the barkeep.

Then we wait, minutes later I pull again and still later again only this time I do not stop yanking on the cord. Eventually we hear the scrape of the key turn; the clang of the bars being pulled back and the door squeaks open outlining the barkeeper standing there in his night clothes. From his surprised expression it is obvious that he was not expecting to ever see us again but the look of genuine relief when he sees just us on the other side of the door is comical.

Ever the businessman his first words are, "Would you like rooms it is very late? I also have some stew left over for a bit of a meal if you would like but I'd have to warm it up for you."

Horatio flips him the coin he had promised and Mistress replies, "We'll just take rooms tonight, we have some of our own supplies still, but a beer or two would not go amiss. I should also say that soon you will be receiving a guest from beyond that door. A guest, I must add who it would be a very good idea to deal with fairly as he is going to be around for a very long time."

The barkeep looks a bit worried but shows us to some rooms that are good for the night, even if the inn does not have those lovely tubs other bars have. Mistress goes one way and at her nod I follow Horatio to a different room where we both collapse in sheer exhaustion.

Chapter Twenty

I had literally been stomping back and forth across my floor grinding my teeth, Boyo is hiding in some corner of my house and even the guards have decided it might be a very good time to patrol the outside. As my hell-phone goes off, I flip it open with such a snap I almost break the casing. Seeing it is my Slut and I demand, "Where are you MINE?" in a deadly voice.

"On my way to you now Mistress this devoted slave has just been returned."

"Good! Come here directly, if any stop you tell them, your Mistress Baroness Spite of Pandemonium wants you home NOW!" With a violent flip I close the case once more and take some deep breaths. I know from past experience that a summoning could be a very random thing and could snatch a person away from all sorts of endeavors. But the thing that keeps nagging at me is that I tested her and my slave can have no cult now, no-one should be able to summon her as her morals are too high to be summoned by a Succi and too low for an Inq. That combined with Mistress's strange statement about her being purple? This is plainly bizarre, when summoned, all Succis are red and all Inq's are blue, so what is this purple? If it had come from anybody but Mistress it simply would not be believable as anything more than a lie or a hallucination.

At last I see her coming through the door and scurrying up to kneel in front of me, she has every appearance of being nothing more than a new and now devoted slave.

"You will explain yourself Slut. You will not voice a single untruth even if you feel it may hurt you or I, is that clear?"

"Yes Mistress, your slave will hide nothing. Your slave knows very little except that there is now a new cult and your slave was chosen by an unknown Demigod who claimed to make her the demonic head of the Druidic cult."

I cough once, "Either this is the worst lie I have ever heard or something very strange is going on. I will not punish you for lying until I know for sure what has happened."

"Mistress please your slave will not lie to you, she wants only to please and serve you. When she arrived in London she was neither red nor blue but purple, she met a Demigod named Creighton along with Mistress Copper and others. She was told she was now the High Demoness of the Druidic order; she was even given a new spell book that contains many common spells as well as spells that are new. This is how she arrived from Elysium. Finally the Demigod put his own Hell-phone number in the phone Mistress gave this demoness and made it speed dial number three. His last instructions were to give the phone to you so he could explain directly to you."

I am aghast my new slave has not connected that many words since I took her. That is one thing but what she is saying is really something else again. A new cult! I reel, my slave as the demonic head of a cult of tree huggers! Trying to make sense of this I ponder will this make her the highest noble of her kind? She would probably be at least a 'High Lady'. How can a Baroness of one cult hold the leash of the leader of another?

What will this do to my own nobility? The new spells, a new Demigod this is all just too huge a gulp to take in at one time.

Mistress had said that the game was afoot but this is becoming something much larger with many more sinister echoes than the distant stompings of a bunch of smelly feet.

In resignation I take the Hell-phone from her and press speed dial number three if only to find out if this is at last, the time for the whole shit house to go up in flames.

Chapter Twenty one

Wrapped in each other's arms still wearing the protective and enhancing amulet I can almost believe that our dreams were similar but I could not have proven it even to myself as our sleep was so deep. When we wake it is to Dovey shaking us and telling us to, "Stir our stumps!" Reluctantly we climb out and longingly look at our love nest only to be admonished with, "Rumpy pumpies will be even better at home than away".

Hurry and then hurry some more seems to be the plan for the day as not only I but everyone can feel Mistress's impatience to get home. So with barely enough time to gnaw on some hard dried meats and the last of the trail mix we are off.

Just as I am about to lead us onto the path Sugar comes to me, "Cyril will be getting some practice tracking, trailing and following unseen, so please sister don't burn my pupil, just save your charges for the feathered fiends." I just grin then wave to Cyril as he moves back from the party to behind the Inn. At a nod from Mistress I step onto the road stretch my senses out, spin and blow a bloody bird off the gables of the Inn. The Medallion! I swear it is making it not only much easier to detect them but this time I even realize that the bird is not actually being commanded or directed it just records what it sees. How I know that I'm not sure but the medallion almost gives me enough enhancements to see what the bird has seen. I know the information is there I just can't quite touch it. Standing quizzically looking up for a minute attracts Mistress's attention beyond just my response to the bird.

"Is there a problem MINE?" Mistress asks.

"No Mistress but this medallion makes finding the birds so much easier that I can almost understand them now." She nods and I turn back to the road in front of me. Moving quickly not wanting to waste time we almost trot down the forest trail as easily as a street in town. The warm morning sun beating down in front of me is creating lovely dusty streamers of light between the trees. Occasionally I glimpse the shadow of someone off to my left and grin at the thought of Cyril still learning one of his new endeavors. I have traveled for less than an hour when I signal a stop for a quick drink of water. Raising my flask I hear a shoe scuff to one side, thinking it is Cyril I casually turn only to encounter armed men attacking us from both sides. Dropping the flask I try to use my wand but a sword knocks it from my hands as another sword is at my throat.

I freeze, everyone else has at least one or two Inq warriors on them but not a drop of blood has been shed yet. A tall dark armored figure holding Mistress by the hair and pressing a Silver Dagger to her throat commands, "Drop your weapons or she dies this instant!"

Horatio shouts his own charge, "Stand down! I order you as Inquisitor General!" But no one obeys instead several smile and even laugh.

An older grizzled man with short cropped salt and pepper hair steps out of the trees and begin to sneer, "Go ahead and order away Inquisitor General but instead of obeying you, you are going to be the first Inquisitor General to be executed on the rack as a traitor. That will be after you and the red headed whore see her slaves and your hooker friends have their hearts torn out, when you have seen all that and more, I'll personally cut your heart out myself, you disgusting whoremonger."

Horatio looks at the assembled Inq's with disgust and dismay, "You have been seduced by evil! You will destroy all we have stood for. For what is being done today you will be hunted by all true Inq's" But as his eyes see Jansen his jaw drops, "Jansen have you gone mad, you're better than this, you could be a mighty Inq, I choose, trained and raised you to your station myself. How can you do this thing?"

Mistress ignores the Inq dagger pressing at her throat just focuses on the old man, I feel her as she turns white her mind a ball of shock, rage and hatred for the one I know now to be Malthus. The man who has his blade on my throat is Horatio's own aide Jansen; he totally ignores Horatio and merely smiles pleased with himself in anticipation of the upcoming events. All of the Inquisitors seem to be jovial almost festive at our bloodless capture.

Malthus goes up to Hex and pulls her hood off before pressing a blade to her face, "Copper you will tell your whores to get down on their knees or I'll cut this one's eye out. Do it now bitch!"

I felt Mistress's horror but her rage is complete. "Never will I order MINE to kneel to that which is not worth pissing on." Hex's screams as her eye is gouged out with the tip of a dagger, abruptly her screams end as she falls back unconscious from the pain and horror.

Malthus leaves Hex to her miseries and goes to Mistress. "Slaves you will kneel now or watch me cut your Mistress to bloody bits! The rest of you will get your chance to die as well. He then walks over to Dovey pinching her cheek gleefully gloating, "Or perhaps I will let you repent as I carve pieces of bacon from you."

I drop to my knees I just cannot endanger Mistress. Every one of the family also kneels we have no choice. Horatio, Dovey and Slice stand, I swear to myself if I ever have the chance this man will scream as he slowly dies by my hand. He walks away from Mistress, comes over to the front of the party and casts a spell. Before him appears a torture rack, the preferred way for an Inquisitor to sacrifice a Succubus.

He turns to me, "You are the whoring little slut that led my pupil to his doom, for that the new Demigoddess's of 'The New Order of Inquisitors' has suggested that you be the first I sacrifice to her; you will be the first to feel a New Inquisitor's blade cut your heart form you. Jansen, because you were my inaugural follower and because you freed me, you have earned the right to do the honors here so now I command you as your new Inquisitor General to rid the world of this discussing little whore?"

As Jansen drags me to my feet I spit in Malthus's face saying, "My death will not save you, for the world is about to change you piece of filth."

Jansen continues to hold me as Malthus slaps me, my teeth rattle in my head, he snarls at me but I laugh in his face and feel a surge of pride from Mistress. I remembered her whip and the tree; I remembered the pain being redirected and have an idea. "Coward you send a boy to do your dirty work! What's the matter getting too old as well as too fat and stupid?"

In the corner of my eye I see Horatio struggle against his captor and be beaten to the ground for his troubles. My own frustration is building into rage that I have to free. "You are a disgusting old fool you have no more right to draw your next breath than a piece of bird shit." I remember then his fear of birds as he grabs me and forces me onto the rack chaining my hands and ankles wide. The rage in his face is easy to see and I know I am about to die but I am not going alone. "You're going to meet the big bird. That's right, the big bird is going to come down and peck your head off."

I see the ritual dagger raised above my head and begin its downward arc. I see the sun glint off the blade but look into his eyes and focus fully on the medallion and Malthus, praying I can drive the pain and shock of the attack right back at him. Impact but the knife bounces back falling from Jansen's hand, I cannot breathe I try to gasp but there is no air in my lungs the violent force of the blow has brutally thrust me back into the torture rack. Malthus hands the knife back to Jansen and having regained my breath I laugh at them both. I had seen him stagger when Jansen tried to kill me. "Malthus you are a bird brained, worthless, weakling, you cannot sacrifice even the lowliest Succi." I laugh again at him. Mistress is there in the back of my mind trying to give me strength, she does not know what has happened but is trying desperately to help. As Jansen raises the dagger to try again, I spit in his face. I sense joy in Mistress but focus on Malthus as the dagger falls once more. Again it bounces back and this time Malthus is knocked to the ground but this time the medallion shatters.

Malthus rolls over as shouts of a melee breaking out are heard behind us. Cyril has a garrote around the throat of the man who had held Mistress captive, he turns himself twisting his hands and hunching forward pulling the man onto his back. The garrote rips through flesh and bone causing the man's head to fall to the ground.

Sugar slips up unseen behind Jansen as only an assassin can, resembling an avenging angel of death her arms spread out and back like wings, she attacks by slamming forward to drive all of the six blades of her pair of new knives directly into his brain and spine. Both of the central blades of her triple bladed daggers drive in through his ears while the shorter blades bite through his temples and spine. His death is instantaneous.

I hear the welcome crack of Mistress's whip like sweet music in my ears as she tries to fight her way to me. Dovey leaps in the air spinning with her tutu fully extended tearing her captor's guts into hamburger as she screams, "I'm short, I'm fat, and I'm proud of that! And YOUR bacon is MY breakfast!"

Malthus dropping his sword runs into the forest as I struggle to break free of the rack, with me yelling curses and calling him a coward as he flees. The rest of the inquisitors are either fighting against rapidly increasing odds, or dead and dying. Horatio, mouth in a grim straight line is silently crying as he tears his sword out of a man's belly then hacks at another of his former comrades. Thankfully Sugar no longer having an opponent worthy of her skills comes to me and sets her nimble fingers to the task of freeing the chains from my wrists and ankles as they unlock, the magically conjured torture rack dissolves into dust and I fall to the ground. Automatically reaching for my wand I crouch looking for a target but to my disappointment see none standing and with a sigh I sit back and survey the carnage.

Seeing Mistress and Cyril with Hex, I feel ashamed that I had been so caught up in my own plight that I had completely forgotten Hex's horror. Mistress is crying over her holding her gently but Cyril is taking out his new wooden book. Reading and flipping pages frantically looking for something he wants then smiles in satisfaction at Hex. Taking out his sprig of Mistletoe, he kisses her bloodied eye socket before whispering syllables that are more forest sounds than words. A sudden gust of wind rustles and swirls all around them swirling, whipping dust everywhere. I hear Hex gasp in astonishment and feel happy delight from Mistress.

Cyril looks up in satisfaction at everyone, "I guess 'Old Boney' from the maze really did give me a calling of some worth, I wish I could have helped sooner but I would have failed unless everyone was looking away. So when they concentrated on Doll I attacked. Sugar taught me the assassination style well but as he died I knew I had sent him to hell and his soul now resides in my garrote." Looking back at the severed head of the man who had attacked Mistress, "That will make a fine trophy, when I locate a place to work from."

Surprisingly he starts to laugh to himself almost uncontrollably then turns and grinning at all of us, "You know, I don't want to give away any secrets or dispel someone else's illusions but I only had to kiss Hex's eyes to restore them, just as Sugar could have been kissed, felt the droplet of a single tear, or even drank Creighton's blood, for it is a fluid from a druid that makes it all work. Mind you after 300 years I can understand his choice. Now if you don't mind I'm going to leave you. I may be able to track that two legged monster to where ever his lair is, I have a spell or two that can aide me, if I do find him I'll contact you for now we all have reason to see him ended." With these words Cyril walks to the tree line waves to us and silently vanishes into the forest.

Sugar looking after him muses with a small smile, "Anyone that looks as good as he did can have a blow job any time he likes even if I don't need healing."

I am still shaking with anger but Slice and Dovey are busily collecting prize pieces from the corpses. Horatio is sitting at the side of the road in a state of dejection; as Cum, Taken, Crap and Sugar resume their prowl searching for any sign of anything that might even look like a dream of hostility. Going over to Horatio I do not need to be empathic to understand his pain, for he has been betrayed by his own aide and some of his comrades have turned out to be traitors. I stoke his hair but do not say a word and find this comforting to myself as well; I will just be here for him when he is ready.

As usual it is Mistress who takes command urging us to head home. Horatio stands beside me and as I look up at Mistress I hear her say, "Taken you are on point now Doll needs a break." I smile in gratitude but as I hold on to Horatio the realization of what had almost happened to me finally hits. My knees go weak and I start to shiver uncontrollably even though the hot late morning sun is beating down. It becomes a real question of whether I am helping; being helped or perhaps the two of us are just moving together sharing the shock of the morning. Horatio and I keep putting one foot in front of the other moving forward through the forest and then the streets.

Onlookers gape as they see us, drenched in blood, armor rent and torn with patches and dents, literally propping ourselves up, all of us have been pushed to the limit and it shows. But what we do not show is defeat, we may be dirty, grimy and blood soaked, well all of us except Horatio who is as clean as the day we left Oxford but our heads are high. Every step we take seems to add to our pride in what has been accomplished. Soon a group of followers is crowding in asking questions and some even offering to help.

That is until we turn the corner that takes us to Mistress's House. There it is Taken who sounds the alarm. Mistress's home is on a usually quiet back street but the road is now jammed with people all talking at once. Many people are milling around looking at a doorway that has been blasted apart. Seeing this, the others all run and charge through the crowd, brutally pushing away those in front of them. Horatio and I are right behind and come out of the crowd directly in front of the ruined doorway there laying in the street being helped by a woman I had never seen is Pepper; she lay there unconscious with bruises over half her head. I hear someone say 'Robo-Cops' and feel Mistress's shock and rage.

In a trance I step away from Horatio; that is my sister lying there, someone said she is still alive but that is not the point. I look at Mistress's house; see the burned gaping hole that used to be a doorway, a now violated doorway to the home of my Mistress. I remember Pepper her bubbly kindness and caring as I check my supply of charges. I turn to Crap and grab her dagger. I just start walking. I am going to kill Robo-Cops!

They attacked, they are the enemy and they are now my prey. I feel a bird flying and spying; casually I blow it out of the air without even looking and start pushing through the crowd.

Vaguely I hear Horatio's voice coming through the crowds saying, "Doll Stop! Don't go alone!"

Slice hollers very loud, "Not now Doll!"

Pure pain breaks through my red hazed rage as Mistress's whip tears through the mail on my back.

Suddenly Mistress is in front of me screaming, "Get on your knees girl!"

As though coming out of a trance I quickly drop to my knees and hear.

"As MINE you stand! As MINE you fight! And As MINE we conquer! You shall never forget that again! Now say it after me."

Looking fixedly up at Mistress feeling the full force of her rage through my bond, my own rage drowned in hers. I lower my head and whimper into her war sandals, "Yes Mistress. As MINE your slave will stand!

As MINE your slave shall fight!

And As MINE your house shall conquer!" Finally reverently I add, "For you Mistress!"

www.ingramcontent.com/pod-product-compliance
Lightning Source LLC
Chambersburg PA
CBHW031313120626
46554CB00001BA/384